PRAISE FOR JOHN CLEVELAND

"John Cleveland has done it again, with a thought provoking, sometimes heart wrenching, and soul-searching novel about us...human beings...God's children. You will find yourself cheering for Helly and the Chinese Buddhist monks who raised her, and the American couple who took her in. You will laugh as Helly learns our odd American customs and teenage slang. You will cry and get angry at our frequently immoral and debased culture. But in the end, you will applaud and rejoice as our human spirit overcomes its fear and does the right thing. A great read!!!

- SCOTT COTTRELL, AUTHOR OF *WHEN CHAOS REIGNS*

This captivating novel beautifully weaves the tale of a kind-hearted girl raised by Shaolin monks, whose grace and inner strength shine through every challenge she faces. The author's vivid storytelling brings to life the serenity of the monastery and the chaos of modern America in striking contrast. Her journey to reconnect with her lost family is both heartwarming and deeply inspiring, filled with moments of wisdom and quiet resilience. A rare blend of martial arts, cultural depth, and emotional discovery, this book leaves a lasting impression.

- ANDY LEBLANC, REVIEWER

In Steeped in Shaolin, author John Cleveland brings readers a compelling fusion of Eastern philosophy and contemporary storytelling. With a deep appreciation for discipline, resilience, and human connection, he crafts the unforgettable journey of Helly—a girl raised in a secluded monastery and thrust into the complexities of modern American life. His storytelling is rich in spiritual insight and emotional depth, asking readers to reflect on identity, purpose, and the quiet strength found in self-discovery.

I found it hard to put the book down—each chapter pulled me in deeper, and I didn't want to stop reading. John writes with such clarity and feeling that you can't help but root for the characters and question your own journey along the way.

- BECKY MASON, REVIEWER

Steeped in Shaolin grabs you by the gi on page one and draws you through teenage brawls, secret emails, and kiss-in-the-park surprises faster than you can shout "hi-ya!" The author wields a black-belt gift for holding your attention while scattering valuable, relevant nuggets on courage, friendship, and faith like fortune cookies tossed into a whirlwind—snag one and you'll snap to the next page just to see what cracks open next. I couldn't put it down.

- KYLE HILL, AUTHOR OF *THE BULLETPROOF AND UNBREAKABLE MARRIAGE*

John intricately weaves a suspenseful, heartwarming, thought provoking story that is tough to put down. Like an episode of a great show with a precipitous end that leaves me eager to find out what happens next, I found myself disappointed that I couldn't binge the sequel immediately!

Steeped in Shaolin is an engaging story filled with thought provoking themes. There are moments of depth and comedy throughout the uniquely written cross-cultural adventure.

STEEPED

IN

SHAOLIN

John Cleveland

Published by JC Writing

ISBN-13: 979-8-9988931-1-7

Cover design by: Sam Designer
Printed in the United States of America

CONTENTS

I

II

This book is dedicated to every young woman (or young man) who puts the safety and well-being of others before their own.

Fear is for others.

- BRUCE LEE

INTRODUCTION

Girls are different. There. I've said it. The mere mention of this idea has ruffled a lot of feathers recently, but it shouldn't. Women are unique, mysterious, fascinating creatures that (if you believe the Bible is true) were the pièce de résistance of creation.

The hero in our story is actually a heroine. Although she might have chosen a different path, the events of her life quite literally fling her into a crucible that will strengthen and refine her to an amazing degree. However, to the casual observer, she is unassuming, pretty, sweet, meek and polite.

Steeped in Shaolin asks the questions:

- *Is there room within us to be something else?*
- *Are we so locked into our patterns of life that we are blind to opportunity?*
- *Might there be moments where we need to color outside of the lines?*

Life doesn't wait for you to be ready. It throws challenges and choices in your path, just as it does for our heroine and her friends. Their journey could be happening right now – around you, in the real world. So, take a deep breath, grab your nunchucks and prepare for Steeped in Shaolin.

PROLOGUE

Tuesday Morning – Maple Ridge Greenway

Serpents have a tendency of peeking. Silently and slowly, they slither out from their holes as they survey the surroundings for prey. Likewise, Dustin carefully peered out from around the edge of the large oak tree. His dark clothes blended in with the forest background, and the sun had not yet risen enough to illuminate his position. He had a perfect view of the paved path that wound through the park and down the slope before disappearing into the tunnel beneath the service road. It would be a perfect ambush. A rush flourished through his veins as the inevitability of his prey's arrival drew closer. *This is what hunters must feel like right before pulling the trigger,* he thought.

This would not be a crime of opportunity. In his warped and deceived mind, he had convinced himself that it wasn't really a crime at all. It was the righting of an injustice. He had been cheated by life, circumstances and even fate. This stalk was also the result of weeks of watching, planning and waiting. As he recalled all of the preparation, a random thought interrupted his focus. *If I had devoted this much time and effort to a real relationship, I probably could have had a real girlfriend by now.* Shame, frustration and anger filled his brain as he shook away the intrusion.

Focus. She'll be coming around the corner any moment. He looked at his watch for the dozenth time. It was 6:12 AM.

Historically, she arrived at the park at 6:05 AM, stretched for about a minute and then began her run. It had been like clockwork, two or three days each week, either Monday, Wednesday and Friday, or Tuesday and Thursday. It alternated with the same consistency. As he waited, he visualized her smooth toned legs, her petite frame, her dark brown hair always pulled back into a high ponytail. He craved her like a dog salivating over a steak. There was also that look of determination. Her eyes were always focused on the path about twenty feet ahead of her, never looking to the right or to the left, and certainly not up to the shaded tree line where he waited on this cool, autumn morning.

His heart almost doubled its rhythm. *There she is*. His quarry had appeared. She rounded the curve, alone, her running shoes lightly pounding the pavement with the accuracy of a metronome. How sweet this would be. He couldn't wait to grab her from behind, put the knife to her throat and dare her to scream. Her eyes would go wide with terror and that smug confidence that she portrays would fracture into a mask of fear. She would fear him. She would respect him. She would submit to him.

He looked left and right to make sure the coast was clear before leaving his shadowy concealment. She was trotting down the grade and nearing the darkness of the tunnel. He picked up speed and closed the distance quickly. He tightened his grip on the knife and mentally practiced the move one more time.

The far end of the tunnel opened to a shady area where neglected trees and shrubs hung over the path. From there, it would be a short drag down to the stream's edge where sounds would be muffled and privacy was assured.

x

Fueled by adrenaline, he covered the remaining ten feet between them. To be this close to her in person, he was surprised by how small her frame was. He was at least 10" taller and probably twice her weight. *All the better. Easy prey.*

It went exactly according to plan. Right arm across her chest, left hand holding the knife against the neck, medium pressure, not enough to break the skin but enough to ensure immobility, silence and cooperation. He pulled her back to his chest and easily lifted her off the ground. In his adrenalized state, she felt unusually light. He moved to the right under the cover of pine branches and began to negotiate the gentle downgrade covered in pine straw. To his great relief, she didn't struggle or scream. *So far, so good.* His heart was pounding with excitement.

A faint signal of caution registered somewhere in his mind, but it was not immediately heeded. Only when she spoke did it garner his attention.

"Are you confident of your success?" It was her. She was eerily monotone, emotionless, or maybe even bored. Her voice was so quiet as to be barely audible, but for some reason it filled him with the same punch of dread that a close lightning strike instills. His knees suddenly felt weak.

"Excess size can be a snare in warfare. You should reconsider." Again, that nonchalant attitude. Completely indifferent. *What is going on here? What is wrong with her? Maybe she has some type of emotional condition where she's unable to express fear?* Whatever it was, it was becoming very unnerving. He had expected her to panic, cry and even beg for her life. He had envisioned having total control of the situation, complete dominance. But now, he found himself questioning his position.

PART I

John Cleveland

601 AD, SHAOLIN TEMPLE, HENAN PROVINCE, CHINA

Twelve men sat on the floor with their almost orange robes draped across tightly crossed legs. Each head was shaved and the Asian features of their faces varied mostly by age. Uniformity was a bonding aspect of life in the monastery. As they had arrived at the gates, each had made the choice to live according to this way because of strong internal desires and repulsions. The desire was for simplicity and pureness. The repulsion stemmed from a perpetual dissatisfaction and restlessness. Each had tasted and disliked the pursuit of contentment through accumulation. Today's fashions would become obsolete tomorrow. The finer things not only required storage and maintenance but became the targets of thieves. Wealth was relative and fickle, and somehow led to higher dissatisfaction as it grew. The system of the world was an impossible quandary whose only solution was escape. Hence, the monastery. Each disciple would forfeit ownership of any and all possessions. Heads would be shaved to discourage vanity and individualism. Then began the lifelong process of learning the ways of Buddha Dharma.

Over 1,000 years earlier, these teachings were developed in Northern India and then began to migrate to China. The essence of this way was detaching oneself from this world and perceiving the trials of existence as opportunities for growth. The shedding of human desires required complete sacrifice physically, mentally and emotionally. The process was practiced and refined day after day through a strict and austere regimen. Talking was rare, meditation was almost constant, and every task was performed with purpose and contemplation. Consideration for everyone except yourself was the basis for all decisions.

Hence, the decision facing this council. The temple had been constructed 106 years earlier and had become known as a sanctuary of sacred ways...and lamentably, things. There were statutes, precious metals, works of art and religious artifacts that the monks viewed as hallowed. Weary travelers and refugees found solace in the lavish surroundings. Bandits, however, saw opportunity.

It had happened three days prior that six men snuck into the compound just before daybreak. Brandishing sticks and small knives, they had thoughtlessly invaded the sacred grounds and carried away as much as each man could carry. Monks who positioned themselves at the exits and petitioned the scoundrels to reconsider were struck with the long sticks. They fell to the blows without reprisal and watched as priceless objects of worship disappeared into the surrounding forest.

The council reviewed the testimonies of the events and spent considerable time silently processing what their course of action should be. It was an impossible situation because their whole existence was based on an abandonment of earthly materialism and concern for self. On the other hand, there were ties to this world that were not easily severed. Even the most ascetic monk still needs shelter, food, clothing and safety. How does one avoid the trappings of life while still operating in the theater of human nature?

The first suggestion came from a younger monk who was still somewhat brash by monastery standards. The fact that he voiced his opinion aloud and before anyone else was a testament to this. "Guards should be hired and future intruders should be executed. This is sacred ground which makes us, its inhabitants, sacred as well. Desecration of the holy demands death." No one corrected the young monk. His journey was in its infancy and wisdom would be learned even through this current process. He continued staring at the spot on the floor just ahead of himself, but his eyes were set and his expression reeked of consternation.

A communal pause was observed as the others contemplated his words out of respect. After all, inspiration often arrives from the most unexpected sources. A middle-aged monk spoke up next. He had developed well in the way and was still very idealistic about the world. "We should not protect the items of the temple or our lives. They are the final test of our detachment.

6

Our willingness to lose the things we hold most dearly proves the highest level of devotion." Everyone agreed that this was a beautiful sentiment, but they also understood that its application could mean extermination.

Constant in each man's thoughts was the balance of all things. Extremes were to be avoided. They could neither coldly kill their enemies nor show indiscriminate kindness. The first showed no value of human life. The second neglected the value of each other. Surely there was an obligation to protect the life of a peer. Inaction was an action in itself.

The council continued to ponder and reflect for several minutes. Individual thought processes began to merge into a collective course of action. Finally, the eldest monk spoke up, not to suggest but to announce what they had all decided upon. "The grim task of protecting what we value falls upon us. We will not burden another with this dark responsibility. Let the ferocity of our defense be equal only to our devotion." Each man had come to this conclusion on his own and their silence signaled their consent. They also knew that the process would be endless and evolutionary. Darkness would ebb and flow alongside the population of men. Yin and Yang prescribed and foretold the balance of light that would naturally ensue. Could the use of violence to prevent violence somehow lead to peace?

14 YEARS AGO
SONGSHAN MOUNTAINS,
HENAN PROVINCE, CHINA

The lowest fringes of their amber colored robes seemed to dust the dark soil as they plodded along the trail silently and reverently. Each one walked evenly spaced behind the other with their eyes focused on the heels of the man directly ahead. One would have mistaken them to be inattentive of their surroundings but, in fact, the opposite was true. Devoid of the deluge of distractions which plagued the Western Hemisphere, they were able to tune themselves into their surroundings with an intimacy that rivaled that of an older married couple. Just as a husband and wife of many decades can finish each other's sentences and discern each other's thoughts, the monks had a similar relationship of wordless warmth with these mountains.

The lead monk stopped in his tracks, which caused the others to stop in place. Instead of the expected accordion effect, each maintained his distance as they had while in motion. As a group, they quietly looked around to investigate an awareness that something was out of place. Something was here that had not been here before. Something was here that did not belong.

The second in line was the first to spot the suitcase. The blue, plastic cube was lying on its side on the fern covered slope to their right. It was heavily scuffed and streaked with dirt but otherwise intact. They looked to the fourth man in line, who nodded that it was permissible to investigate. The first two men broke rank and were stealthily moving further into the vegetation when they both suddenly froze.

The suitcase was crying.

With more caution, they resumed their approach. Both men were now moving in a slightly squatted posture as they walked with their elbows slightly flared and hands positioned defensively just ahead of their midsections. It was in these moments that their radical noise discipline

10

seemed justifiable. Automatically, they split apart slightly as if covering the case from two different angles, their eyes locked on the clasp for any movement. The second man knelt slowly and placed his hands on the corners. Perhaps he sensed an absence of danger through some honed sensitivity in his hands because he slid them over the locks and released each button. As he opened the case, there were the expected pants, shirts, underwear and socks. But there was also a little face. Its blue eyes blinked at the strangers. Tears streamed down red cheeks outlined by skin that was several shades lighter than that of the men. A *Westerner,* the monk correctly deduced to himself. She was perhaps three years of age and appeared to be more scared than injured. He noticed a small amount of blood on the front of her shirt but could not see its source.

In their way of life, surprises were rare. Mysteries were part of existence and the known must be balanced by the unknown. The extreme temperance of their demeanors allowed them to consider the situation reasonably. If their thoughts had been audible, they would have begun with the obvious and branched out from there following the most logical path of possibilities. *The child could not have entered and locked the case on her own. Placing her in the case could have been for punishment but was more likely for protection. No one carries a suitcase of this size by hand into these mountains. This suitcase was delivered here by a modern form of transportation and an airplane is the only viable mode considering the terrain. The case is not fractured so it did not fall from a great height.*

The other monk had silently drawn the same conclusion, as had the other monks waiting in their domino-esque formation back on the trail. Their communal deductive reasoning could almost be mistaken for telepathy. Each began to look upward on the higher slopes to see if anything was out of place. Moments later, the fourth monk actually spoke in his native language.

He turned to the third monk and gave instructions. "Lead the others to the crash site. We will take the child to the monastery and wait for your report." Without questions or protest, he joined the two monks who had inspected the suitcase. These three men formed a new line and then moved down the trail at a slightly quicker pace before veering off on a new one that inclined steeply to their right.

The remaining three convened around the child, who now sat bewildered in the open suitcase. Her mouth was pouting beneath drooping, glassy eyes. In her young state, she searched the faces of those surrounding her for relief from her anguish. Uncertainty and loss were evident in her eyes. The permanence of the latter was not yet fully realized. The men lowered themselves onto their haunches and assumed open yet passive body positions. They crossed their legs in what American children once called "Indian style" until it was deemed offensive. They laid their forearms on their knees and held their palms upward. They did not stare at the child but casually looked about and at each other. When the child was ready, she would reach out.

In less than a minute, she did. She extended her hands toward the elder of the group and offered a cry of need. He reciprocated and extended his hands until they were under her little arms. He gently removed her from the rumpled collection of clothing and drew her close to his robe. She then wrapped her arms around his neck and placed her cheek near his collar bone. The human touch was not equal to her mother's, but it was more than adequate to stave off the sting of her ordeal.

14 YEARS AGO
EARLIER THAT SAME DAY, SONGSHAN
MOUNTAINS, HENAN PROVINCE, CHINA

The Cessna 172 is the quintessential small workhorse aircraft. Almost 45,000 had rolled off of the assembly line since its introduction in 1955. Affordable, dependable and versatile, it had served in almost every capacity possible all over the globe. In less regulated countries, it was often asked to exceed its design parameters, especially in terms of its gross weight capacity. If weighed on a scale, it should never exceed 2,500 pounds during take-off. This prescribed limit is further affected by altitude, temperature and weather conditions. But like an overloaded burrow, the little 172 could be whipped and prodded into the air. With its engine screaming, it would strain against and obediently defy gravity even when its owner should have been more considerate.

Such was the case that morning when the Nepalese pilot refueled the aircraft at an airstrip in the nearby town of Zhengshou. His chartered customers took the opportunity to stretch their legs and let their little girl burn off some energy. She looked like a doll version of her mother, who was only becoming more lovely at her present age of twenty-eight. Although only 5'1", Mary was perfectly proportioned and the had the muscle tone of a gymnast. A source of envy to most other women, her face had the proper spacing and agreeable contours that made her stand out in a crowd. The only qualities that outshined her physical beauty were her selfless spirit, kind heart and humility.

Her husband, Jeff, almost matched her attractiveness with his tall, athletic build and bright smile. At thirty-years of age, his intelligence and natural charisma could have taken him down almost any path of life he chose. However, he had politely declined the invitations and opportunities that would have landed him in a six-figure salary career. The accompanying home, car and swimming pool were also demurred. Instead, he had chosen to invest in what he called "eternal savings."

His more than affluent father often thought his life choices were odd but remained supportive nonetheless. Through his connections, Jeff had procured the sponsorship that made these mission trips possible. Truth be told, this handsome missionary was motivated in part by his sense of adventure. Jeff understood that people everywhere needed encouragement and to hear the good news. His evangelistic work could have been performed easily in an American suburb, but where was the excitement in that? Plus, would there be any reception? With dozens of churches to choose from and a televangelist available on multiple television channels, he felt that the U.S. was already saturated with opportunities to know God.

China, however, was not hospitable toward such proselytizing. Had the true nature of their presence been known, the authorities would have hastily escorted them to the nearest international airport where a scornful farewell would have been offered. Any protest of this eviction would likely result in local detainment. With the safety of a young wife and three-year-old daughter always on his mind, he justified the ruse of the "community development" program that allowed them to operate covertly in the tightly controlled country.

The pilot topped off the plane's wing tanks and gave little thought to the weight calculations that should have been completed. At only 371' above sea level, the thickness of the atmosphere was almost optimal for providing lift to the small craft. However, as they climbed to pass over the Mount Song mountain range, the mile of altitude would be just enough to jeopardize their ability to stay aloft.

Sharing the same ignorance as their pilot, Jeff, Mary and their daughter reboarded the 172 and fastened their restraints. The throttle knob was pushed in slightly as they taxied onto the runway and then pushed to its stop as they began to pick up speed. They needed to reach 55 knots, or around 63 mph, before sufficient aerodynamics would lift them from the ground. No one seemed to notice as the speedometer passed 60 knots, then 65 before the front tire reluctantly began to rise. They were passing 70 as the rear tires slowly separated from the pavement. The little girl squealed as her stomach reacted to the suddenly unsupported feeling of flight.

As the town disappeared behind them, a rugged landscape began to materialize ahead on the horizon. The pilot pulled back gently on the yoke, which caused the big and little hand of the altimeter to rotate clockwise. As the plane passed 3,000' and eventually 4,000', its orientation of travel would have been cause for concern to·a more conscientious observer. Instead of climbing a parallel path to their angle of ascent, the tail was slightly dipping and the nose was rising higher. Instead of pulling them forward through the air, the engine was being forced to carry them upward as well. The effect was amplified as they passed 5,000', so much so that the pilot began to make adjustments to the controls. The 172 flailed in a sudden pocket of turbulence and did not recover as quickly as the pilot expected it to. He pushed in the throttle which was already near 100%. He pulled back on the yoke, but the little plane stubbornly refused to comply. He pushed the nose down to try and recover some much-needed airspeed,

19

but another bout of turbulence caused the plane to flounder once more.

A pilot should never transmit worry through his expressions or body language, but apparently he'd missed that day of flight school. It was probably the same day that they discussed cargo capacities. Jeff, sitting in the co-pilot's seat, looked for something to grab onto as the wings dipped and waggled. He thought about grabbing the yoke to offer some assistance or possibly even take over. The fears that passengers typically bar from their minds before boarding a flight suddenly burst through the dam of denial.

"Are we OK?!?" he shouted to the pilot. Without answering, the now sweat-laden man continued to struggle with the controls. Jeff turned to look at his wife who sat wide-eyed in the rear seat, her arms around the little blue-eyed girl strapped in beside her. They exchanged a serious look and chose not to alarm their daughter with any comments. Mary pulled their lap belts tighter and wished that a car seat had been available to them.

Swirling clouds seemed to appear from nowhere. Violent air currents ramped skyward from the steep slopes below. Thermodynamics demanded that rising warmer air would rapidly exchange places with cooler air, which caused the plane to buck wildly. Everyone on board was now praying that God would somehow calm the weather or deliver them safely to the other side.

Mary's protective (and motherly) instincts were activated, which caused her to remove herself entirely from the equation. With reckless resolve, she suddenly unbuckled her lap belt and reached behind the rear seat into the cargo area. A momentary absence of lift dropped the plane 50', which caused her to go weightless and slam into the roof. When the Cessna finally found purchase in the choppy air, she was dropped face first onto the seatback. She heard and felt the bones of her nose break. Neither the warm flow of blood nor pain registered in her mind as she resumed the frantic retrieval of her blue suitcase.

For some reason, the television commercial that had advertised the luggage flashed through her recollection. In the advertisement, they had loaded a dozen eggs inside and then dropped the suitcase from a ten-story building.

When they opened the case, the eggs were all intact. *It will be perfect for China,* she had thought as she reached for the phone and placed an order for the luggage. Now, she thought of the absurdity and possible providence of what she was about to do with the case.

She flipped it open and ripped out her shoes and toiletries. She burrowed a hole in the remaining clothes and then unbuckled the lap belt from her daughter. She thought of how the mother of Moses must have felt when she placed him in the wicker basket. With the swiftness and fierceness of desperation, she placed her daughter in the case. "I love you!" she shouted as she kissed the child on her forehead. As she did, drops of blood from her mother's nose appeared on the front of the girl's shirt. The small eyes widened as she realized what was about to happen.

The little Cessna 172 had fought valiantly but was now spent. After fending off blow after blow, it lowered its wings and offered its chin to the winds. As if preparing for the coup de grâce, the strongest downburst yet forced the plane into a vertical orientation. Anything not fastened down became weightless and clanged around the cabin. The pilot was still uselessly fighting the yoke, which shook and slid above his knees. Jeff was gripping the dash with his right hand and searching the rear compartment for Mary with his left.

The blue suitcase had been firmly latched closed and was bouncing around in the small confines. Mary was now pinned helplessly upside down in the cargo area. The sound that dive bombers make in the movies became very evident to those experiencing the horror of uncontrolled descent. The gauges spun wildly clockwise and counter-clockwise depending on their function. Helplessness led to surrender. Jagged peaks and patches of green filled the view of the windshield as the pilot continued his futile efforts at recovery.

Physics, although invariable in most cases, can yield odd results when coupled with chance. An accident reconstructionist would have given an infinitesimal probability of survival for anyone on board given the factors. These odds held true as the lives of the three adults were snuffed out even before the sound of the impact frightened away the birds nesting in nearby trees. The aluminum alloy airframe was built to be lightweight at the expense of crash resistance. Not that it would have mattered given the speed at impact.

The thick canopy of trees acted like a can opener that savagely sheared off the wings and peeled open the fuselage. As the bodies on board were compacted and twisted, a blue rectangle of reinforced plastic tumbled out of the wreckage and cartwheeled down the trunk of an angled tree, which transferred its velocity from vertical to horizontal. It then tumbled through the low branches and was slowed further by the thicker foliage below. It flipped twice more before landing on the sloping ground, where it slowly slid downhill for over one hundred yards. It finally came to rest in a patch of ferns where, unbeknownst to its occupant, a well-worn walking path passed by just a stone's throw away.

14 YEARS AGO
WEDNESDAY, 5:00 PM, SHAOLIN TEMPLE,
HENAN PROVINCE, CHINA

The monks formed an unusually informal circle around the small child. She sat on a pile of robes that had been hastily bunched together. Everything about this was incredibly incongruous. In a world of order, structure, discipline and solemnity, there was no place for a three-year-old girl. Uncharacteristically, the eldest monk folded his arms across his chest and scratched his chin as he contemplated what the right course of action should be. This was unlike any other situation he'd faced during his fifty-three-year tenure at the temple. The younger monks, who remained in a perpetual state of admiration of their mentor, took the opportunity to mimic his stance and mannerism. It would have made a humorous photo of the little girl looking into the faces of the wisest men this world had to offer, only to see them staring back cluelessly. And thus, the mysterious and universal dissimilarities between the genders illustrated themselves once again.

After what seemed like an eternity, the eldest monk spoke. But instead of a statement, it was a rhetorical question. These were never asked in their simple world of certainty. "What do you do with a little girl who falls from the heavens?"

The other monks further exercised their momentary liberty by audibly grunting and deepening their scowls as one does when deeply problem solving. Had their collective thought processes been available as a transcript, they would have appeared as such: *Surely, the universe delivered her from the accident and into our hands for a purpose. The severity was too great and the odds of discovery were too slim to be considered chance. But a child should be with her family, who now lay interred on the high cliffs. Surely, there must be relatives in the West. But would the local authorities make any effort to find them or return her? And what would she be subjected to in the West? Had her family not made tremendous efforts to escape from that world?*

In the end, the prospect of providence guided them to their final conclusion. The eldest monk spoke. "We will raise her as our own." Momentarily drunk with expressive liberty, eyes widened around the circle and a few gasps were heard. He extended a hand and held it vertically about six inches away from his chest. It was a firm reminder for everyone to recenter themselves emotionally and focus on the daunting task that would consume the next fourteen years of their lives. The Shaolin Temple now had a female resident.

TEN YEARS AGO
SONGSHAN MOUNTAINS,
HENAN PROVINCE, CHINA

Snowflakes fell hypnotically amongst the alpine green cypress trees. A blanket of white had been in place for over a month now. She stretched each step in an effort to match the larger footsteps that her teacher left as he walked two feet ahead of her. As was his newfound custom, he turned his head every few moments to make sure his human shadow was still closely attached. An unsolicited smile forced the corners of his lips upward as he watched her efforts to be like him. A sense of gratitude filled his being as he mused, *It is a gift to know the experience of a father.*

A whole new world of thoughts and emotions had infiltrated his otherwise disciplined deportment over the last three and half years. They caused a continual

28

temptation to introduce a softness that would have never been extended to a male disciple. Boys had been dropped off routinely at the monastery throughout the years. Some had been devoted to service by their parents. Others were left out of desperation with starvation as the likely alternative. Without much consideration, they were quickly assimilated into the culture and fell into the pattern of life as one would expect. But she was different.

Her once pale skin had darkened considerably in the Asian climate, but her obviously Western, female features made her a curious oddity in this world. When a young boy would make a mistake or carelessly break an object of value, there was immediate discipline and correction. Although it occurred with her, the edge of harshness was dulled ever so slightly. It was a double standard that no man at the monastery had been able to master.

He decided to take a rest break before beginning the steepest part of the trail. As he stopped, she automatically stopped in place. As he turned, he saw her struggle to maintain her balance in the deep postholes his steps had made. Another smile.

"Describe your sensations, Helly."

Helly was not actually the name her parents had given her. However, the shirt she had been wearing upon discovery had "Helly Hansen" embroidered over the left chest. They naturally assumed this was her first and last name. Helly paused to contemplate the query and formulate her words before speaking, which had become her custom. Her eyes looked down and to the right and then to the left. Answering naturally in Chinese, she replied, "My hands have almost no feeling left, nor does my nose. The snowflakes tickle my cheeks and get caught in my eyelashes. I am excited to be on an outing with you and anxious to see what we will discover."

This exercise was meant to strengthen mindfulness in the young child. In developed countries, people's minds were always thinking about the future: things they wanted, things they wanted to happen, things they didn't want to happen. Or they were stuck in the past: *If only I had done this. If only I had followed my instincts. If only things had turned out differently.*

Of course, these were useless musings in the world of

the Shaolin. The past, the present and the future were all intertwined and guided by a universal current. Mistakes, tragedies, and good fortune all conspired to shape each of us into who we were always meant to be. Resisting this current and going against the flow of this cosmic river was ultimately counter-productive. Instead, students were trained to focus on the here and now. This was the secret to their focus.

"Are you ready?" he asked.

She strained to suppress a smile as she gave a militant nod. This slight expression of emotion would not have been acceptable with a male trainee, but...

They continued their slow trudge up the slope.

NINE YEARS AGO
SHAOLIN TEMPLE,
HENAN PROVINCE, CHINA

A row of would-be warriors stood facing the exterior wall of the temple as their instructor paced by in a deliberate and measured fashion. Their eyes did not blink or deviate as his image passed through their individual lines of sight. Each stood adorned in flowy clothing with bright orange folds that made it difficult to discern if it was a shirt, pants or robe. The footwear had the appearance of a sock with a thin, flat sole and black straps that wound around the ankle up to the shin.

Their teacher towered over them, not because he was a giant, but because they were small in stature. Studying each face and shaved head, he affirmed their uniformity of having dark almond shaped eyes, until one did not. The blue eyes had the hue of the Caribbean and the roundness of a doll. Even at this young age, the features of the face were softer and more compact. All of this was framed by dark brown hair that was pulled back tightly into a clasp, which allowed the remainder to fall down past small shoulders. As he passed by, the instructor paused his pacing and frowned. His expression was not born of disappointment but confusion. This was rare in his world and in his thoughts.

The order of the Shaolin had proceeded much the way it had for centuries. Like the hands of a clock that dutifully followed their course day after day, the inhabitants of the monastery were content to exist in a world of simplicity and predictability. Behavioral patterns and emotional responses were never surprising and there had been little need for adaptation. Suddenly, with the arrival of Helly, a small beam of sunlight had revealed that the sky had, in fact, been slightly overcast for what seemed like all eternity.

When not actively training, the other male trainees stared curiously at her and never had the courage to initiate contact. Although her physical presence was smaller, it was as if she possessed a mysterious power that had an assailable effect on everyone who possessed a Y chromosome. Her presence emanated a chemistry that had the ability to disrupt the male train of thought and to tempt even the most stalwart of lips to turn up at their corners when she was around.

"Humph." The teacher regained his composure and resumed his pacing as he began to deliver his instruction. "Each of you is blessed to be standing here in the sibiānxing amongst your peers. The man-," he paused and corrected, "person standing to your side will become the family that you thought you had lost. The inner strength you develop will cause fear and weakness to become a distant memory like that of a dream that dissolves in the waking light. The life force that you possess has the unique opportunity to be cultivated, unified, shared and multiplied." Reaching the terminus of the stone quadrangle, he performed an about-face and continued his speech as he retraced his steps.

"The chisels that will be used in shaping you are the following: discipline, consistency, patience, integrity and above all, selflessness. Your heart does not beat merely

34

for the sake of itself but for the function of the entire body. It does not have to be told to work, but joyfully and faithfully supplies life giving blood and oxygen to its fellow organs. Likewise, we perform our duties for the benefit of the entire entity." Stopping, he turned toward his audience, who remained rigidly locked into a form of "attention" with their eyes peering straight ahead. "Each of you is a tiny but valuable part of that entity. As it is with the body you possess, you would not surrender any natural part of it willingly. Each digit and appendage perform a function and the absence of any of them would reduce your efficacy."

The instructor looked down as if contemplating whether or not he should introduce the next topic. Inhaling as he looked up, he spoke. "Considering that we are parts of a larger organism, we must also be vigilant to prevent and remove parasites. In the context of society, a parasite is he-," (cutting his eyes toward Helly) "or she who acts in a manner that disregards the comfort, provision or well-being of others. Like the invasive growth within a body that gorges itself while depriving the organs of much needed nutrients, they must not be allowed to continue."

His voice took on an edge of hostility. "The rogue will not need to be hunted. They will identify themselves in either a brash or subversive manner. You will be prepared to recognize and react to either circumstance. You will be equipped to perform this necessary and noble task. You will have the skill, strength and stamina to accomplish this." His tone increased in rhythm and intensity. "You must protect the organism to which you are irrevocably infused." He stopped and silence filled the enclosed training area. "Look to your left and your right."

The trainees did as they were told and rotated their heads left and right to examine their peers. The boys on either side of Helly appraised her with curiosity and a fair amount of unease. She observed them with indifference. In her young eyes, they were merely smaller versions of all she had ever known. However, deep in the recesses of her adolescent mind, she had an understanding that there was a species that existed in a similar but also contrasting manner. She already suspected that those belonging to that species could mimic, sometimes with greater effort, most any activity that the males could perform intrinsically. She also sensed that they possessed an almost mystical insight and considered matters from the heart as opposed to the mind. She also realized that she belonged to that species.

"Center!" the instructor commanded, which brought every face forward and caused any ponderings to flee. He looked down the line in each direction to verify compliance before bowing slightly. Each student bowed respectfully in return.

EIGHT YEARS AGO
SHAOLIN TEMPLE,
HENAN PROVINCE, CHINA

A deep but controlled breath escaped through pursed lips. Her eyes remained locked on her opponent as she returned to the pose which allowed for a reset. Breaks in combat were inevitable and useful in reassessing one's strategy. Her lip was swollen and bleeding slightly. The sensation of pain throbbed in her left shin, but it was only categorized and not emotionally acknowledged. She opened her stance by squatting back on her right leg, which was almost behind her at a ninety-degree angle. Her left leg was almost one hundred eighty degrees forward with the foot extended. The right hand was clinched into a fist and held near her right hip. The left hand was held aloft over her right leg about chin height, its palm open and upward.

Her opponent was a boy three years older than she. He was bigger, stronger, more experienced and secretly embarrassed by being paired with a girl. Even in this environment, certain human traits still linger. He was determined to prove that she did not belong here and could never be equal. He lunged fast and fiercely. A stutter step sent his right foot up towards her torso with lightning-fast speed. With reflexes that could only be scrutinized with a slow-motion camera, she brought her right hand under his heel and lifted upward. Her upper body was already bending backwards away from the blow. With his momentum and her unwanted assistance, the boy was losing his footing and performing an unintended backflip. Hers, however, was intentional.

Springing upward with her right leg and kicking the left one forward for momentum, she completed her rotation quickly and landed just in time to close the distance on her fallen rival. He had landed rather clumsily on his stomach but had caught himself with his hands. Unfortunately for him, it was too little, too late. Exposing your back while on the ground was fatal in combat. She dove over him while snaking her arms around his head. Using the momentum of her roll, she pulled his head upward so that he was now in a painful backbend position. She extended her legs and wrapped them in a figure-four around his. She constricted her form and brought his heels within a foot of the back of his head. He let out a squeal of distress that was heard throughout the training area.

"Yield!" The sharp command of an older male voice caused her to instantly disengage and release the other boy from the vise she had created. She snapped to her feet in something similar to a position of attention. Her opponent followed her example, although at a noticeably slower pace, and stood shakily beside her. She was not proud of this victory. She did not feel superior to the older boy. But she felt no sympathy for him either.

FIVE YEARS AGO
SHAOLIN TEMPLE,
HENAN PROVINCE, CHINA

"What is a...colokalism?" Her brow was furrowed as she tried to process and retain the new lesson. Her teacher not only knew English but spoke it with almost no perceivable accent. Before coming to the monastery, he had served as a translator for visiting dignitaries and diplomats. He was a wonderful resource for a young lady who needed some connection to her roots. Unfortunately, his cultural proficiency was a few decades out of date.

With exaggerated slowness and pronunciation, he repeated "Col-lo-qui-al-ism. It is a popular saying that is intrinsic to an area or people group. You may also call it an idiom."

She silently mouthed the strange, six syllable word to herself. She knew that repetition was the key to mastery.

"The first one I will teach you is used to express wonder or delight with a situation. It is *awwe-sooooome.*" Once again, he lengthened and emphasized each section of the word. "This song is awesome."

"Awesome. This song is awesome," she repeated.

"Very good. The next one is similar to the first but contains two words. It serves the same purpose but is simply a variation. *Far out.* That hairstyle is really far out."

Again, her brow furrowed. "But how can a hairstyle be far away? Is the hair not connected?"

He smiled at her naiveté. "These sayings are not meant to be logical, but to compliment or garner acceptance into a foreign crowd."

She complied with the lesson and tried the phrase. "Your hairstyle is very far out."

Close enough, he thought. "The next one is used to imply fondness and can be applied directly to a person. *Groovy. Groooo-veeee.* That girl is so groovy."

"That girl is so groovy." She wanted more information. "But what specifically does groovy mean? I do not want to blindly offer flattery if it is not merited." Life amongst the monks had given her language an inescapable formality.

"To be groovy means to be at peace, easy to like, pleasant in appearance or a combination of all three. It is a high compliment indeed."

She nodded as the information formed connections in the neurons of her brain. Without the barrage of cartoons, toys and gibberish, her mind was optimally open to absorbing data. By virtue of submersion, she was fluent in Mandarin. But the monks knew that the use of English was essential to stay abreast in a rapidly changing world. They also foresaw that it would probably be useful in her future. The past has a way of catching up to us.

"Now, the next one is *dig it*, as in 'I like that shirt. I really dig it.' "

And the confusing lesson continued.

THREE YEARS AGO
SONGSHAN MOUNTAINS,
HENAN PROVINCE, CHINA

The ridge of rock resembled the scales on a dragon's back. The spiny limestone and tightrope of dolomite rock would be impossible to traverse except by the most skilled mountaineers. Chasms hundreds of feet deep fell off sharply on both sides. Her teacher had explained the lesson and its expectations earlier at the temple. In accordance with her training, she had done her best to visualize the described environment and even herself completing the task in her mind's eye. But now, standing on the cold, barren peak, she felt the tendrils of fear seeping into the corners of her concentration. Had she used the word, she would have said that she hated being afraid. However, in their culture, extreme expressions of emotion were not just discouraged but forbidden. Instead, a phrase like "I perceive danger" or "Caution should be taken" was the closest alternative to voicing one's woes. She chose neither, but silently assessed the route she would take across the perilous fin of stone.

Also in her training was the contemplation of death. It was never to be dreaded but should be postponed as long as possible for the purpose of extending one's usefulness. Death was viewed as a natural part of the life cycle and welcomed when the ordained time had arrived. Just like a sunset, not only can it have its own beauty, but it can serve as both a conclusion and a beginning.

Still, her natural sense of self-preservation resisted the image of her tumbling down the slopes and onto the broken shards of talus far below.

Without further prompting, she took a step forward. Her eyes were locked on the area about ten feet ahead where she would be walking. As for her immediate footing, she allowed her subconscious to decipher a path from what her mind had already recorded. Situational awareness was a key to survival.

Slowly and deliberately, she moved across the jagged, vertical edge. Every small motor skill available was currently being devoted to balance. Right as she reached the halfway point, it happened.

"BOOM!!!" A thunderous explosion reverberated through the air about twenty feet to her right. The sky flashed for an instant and was followed by a circle of smoke. She had sunk to a squatting position and rotated toward the blast with her hands held almost vertically about six inches away from her chest. Strangely, her heart rate did not increase perceptibly. Distractions had been a constant part of her training. Although her reflexes had become razor sharp, her emotional reaction to them had become quite dull.

"BOOM!!!" Another explosion behind her, above the opposite chasm. Her young warrior mind was furiously and automatically analyzing threats and prioritizing them. Options were considered and chosen within milliseconds. The objective was to navigate and successfully cross over the narrow ridge. She had already deduced that the explosions were large firecrackers thrown by her teacher.

Aside from being a distraction, they posed no threat. She stood and began to move with the litheness of a cat, eyes focused ahead, hands held at chin level directly ahead. Threat levels vary from moment to moment, and a warrior adjusts their defensive condition accordingly.

She sacrificed some safety for the sake of speed and moved quickly over the remaining distance. Her acutely attuned ears were now scanning for the faint whisper of a lit fuse and the quiet whistling of an approaching projectile. When both of these noises registered anew in her mind, she leapt across a large gap and balanced ever so briefly atop a small pinnacle of rock on her right foot. No sooner had it accepted her weight than it began to shift and slide from its position. Knowing it would not support another leap, she allowed herself to fall forward. The rocky spline rushed up toward her face like an axe, but suddenly it stopped.

BOOM!!! BOOM!!!

The thunderous claps of noise reverberated off of the distant cliffs and returned as slightly muted echoes. Smoke wafted in the air where the girl had been standing a moment before. As it cleared, it revealed the oddest display of gymnastic proficiency imaginable. Two hands were cradling the rock edge below her body, which was seemingly suspended in mid-air. It was as if she were performing a push up without the use of her legs. Each was splayed outward like counterweights. Her tensioned frame rocked slightly in all directions as her muscles fought to stabilize her. The objective had not yet been accomplished, so she slowly lowered her legs as she raised her body. Still supporting herself solely by her hands, she bent her legs like a spider underneath her and tested their grip on the steeply angled rock. With each at opposing forty-five-degree angles, she slowly stood. Once mostly erect, she lept skyward and realigned her feet in midair. Landing lightly on the tightrope of stone, she gracefully completed the last few steps. Upon reaching the level landing of rock on the far side, she turned around and acknowledged her teacher by bowing reverently. For the first time since her training began, he bowed in return.

THREE MONTHS AGO
SHAOLIN TEMPLE,
HENAN PROVINCE, CHINA

Her hands moved fluidly, tracing invisible lines in the space around her. At times, they slowly extended with strongly clenched fists and at others they separated and came to rest open palmed near her sides. Her feet lifted, swiveled and planted in various patterns, each requiring incredible balance and finesse. After completing the routine, she slowly lowered to her knees, pressed her palms together near her chest and closed her eyes. She thought of each of her obligations, and what Americans would call worries, and then slowly exhaled each one out of her lungs like expelled smoke. When her mind and soul were clear of these distractions, she allowed the resulting emptiness to swell and encompass her being. It was in this state that the restorative healing of mental and emotional health could be initiated, thus establishing a clean slate for the day.

An unknown amount of time had passed when she felt a presence enter the small room. She slowly opened her eyes and rose gracefully to her feet so that she could greet whoever it was. She turned and recognized one of her senior teachers, probably the closest thing she had to a father.

Had anyone from the West viewed snapshots of their time together, they would have demanded that he be charged with child abuse, be executed at least a dozen times and then have his ashes blasted into outer space. However, humans have a tendency to make snap judgements based on momentary observations.

For instance, there was the time she stood outside in the snow on a bitter cold winter's day. She was barefoot and wearing only a thin, summer weight robe. Her lips were turning blue as she shivered uncontrollably. Her master stood indifferently six feet away with his arms crossed. He himself was draped in a full-length wool robe with thickly insulated boots made of animal fur. Each hand was warmly tucked into the opposing sleeve of the robe, and a thick,

50

fur lined cap with ear flaps sat atop his shaved head. He was possibly sweating under all of the layers.

She looked up at him, wanting either instruction, reassurance or pity. She knew better than to ask, "How much longer?"

"You are fighting it. You resist the cold. It is fear and discomfort from your mind that currently instructs your body. That is why you shiver."

It had not been instinctual, but she had learned that he was ultimately correct in his lessons. So, she surrendered. She forfeited her discomfort, her concern and her fear. Beginning at once, but taking several moments to complete, her shivering began to abate. After a few more bouts of shaking, she felt her muscles relax. It was only then that she was able to comprehensively perceive and evaluate her condition.

"My feet have no feeling but I can still move my toes. My hands are slow to respond and have no dexterity. My warmth is leaving most quickly through my core and head. It requires concentration and intentionality to speak clear sentences."

Her teacher seemed pleased at her progress and gave the slightest of nods. "On my command, I want you to minister to yourself but without going inside of the monastery. Go!"

Apparently, she had already been mentally improvising ways to stay warm, because she hastily turned and ran off to the woods directly behind her.

He was mildly surprised, as he was expecting her to seek sanctuary around the curtilage of the temple. His curiosity led him to follow her tracks. He followed her into the woods, winding through snow laden branches and finally dead-ending at the top edge of a cliff. He knew that the drop was too high to survive and that she gave no indications of wanting to end her life. Still, he followed the tracks to their terminus and peered over as far as he dared. As he expected, there was pristine snow approximately eighty feet below.

Feeling duped, he retraced his steps, now being more careful to examine the areas to the right and left. However, there were no other tracks. *Clever girl,* he thought to himself. When she was a child, her strategies were predictable and easily thwarted. Apparently, now, not so much. He stopped and became very still so as to absorb everything around him: the sounds, sights, senses and invisible energies that surround each living thing. After a moment, he looked up and noticed that the limbs above him had substantially less snow than other nearby branches. He then noticed upon closer examination that there were fresh indentations in the snow around his feet where larger clumps had recently fallen. He followed the branches with his eyes to a barely noticeable ledge on the cliff face about fifteen feet up on his right.

With amazingly agility for his age, he lithely lifted himself up into the tree until he could see the entrance to what appeared to be a small opening in the cliff face. He also noticed that the limb leading toward the ledge could never hold his weight for more than just a moment. With feline prowess, he crouched with his eyes locked solely on the small step of rock about twelve feet away. It was more like a pounce as he sprung forward and took two quick steps on the narrow branch. Clumps of snow fell to the ground as if to remind him that he would too if he missed his footing. With near silence, he landed gracefully on the tiny rock perch and stabilized himself against the stone wall with his hands.

Peering inside of the opening, he could see flashes of movement and hear grunts of exertion. She was performing something similar to what Westerners would call burpees. Over and over, she dropped into a squat, thrust her legs out behind her and dropped into a push-up. Then, reversing the process, she pushed away from the ground, drew her legs underneath her and then sprung up almost two feet off the ground. Her cheeks were red and her warm breath was coming out in large puffs.

He slid through the opening as she completed a repetition. Registering absolutely no surprise, she bowed toward her teacher while still breathing hard. She had accomplished the objectives resourcefully, discreetly and radically. It had been a much better performance than all of her male peers.

In another instance, she was tasked with fetching water from the well late at night. It was a task she had performed countless times, hoisting the pole onto her shoulders, a bucket hanging languidly from a notch on each end. She had performed this ritual in the heat of summer, the dead of winter and in the darkness of night, so this was not an unusual request. However, when she took a lantern from the table near the door, her teacher gave the command to leave it. The idea of complaining or asking why had become foreign to her, so she turned and walked into the darkness with the empty yoke across her small shoulders.

She walked with her right eye closed, which would stimulate its one million rod cells to activate, thus improving her night vision. In about a minute, when she opened it, she was already much more suited to the dark. In secret, her teacher had staged an ambush on the trail and had instructed the other students to strike as she was returning to the temple. In their adolescence, part of their motivation was fueled by resentment. One by one, the boys had been beaten by her during training and this would be a prime opportunity for revenge. Each suppressed a grin as their teacher had given them the assignment.

They hid along the trail near a section they called "the

grotto." Millennia before, jagged boulders had lodged partially into the ground on both sides of the trail. They formed a miniature amphitheater of sorts with a narrow entrance on one side and a narrow exit on the other. Within the stone walls was a rough circle about twenty feet across. They too had been letting their eyes adjust to the darkness. Not only did they have the same training as her but they had strength in numbers. They had made sure that none of the cadre had followed them, which meant their retaliation would be unobserved and unrestrained.

Each knew from experience the length of time it took to walk to the well, fill the buckets, balance the load and return to this spot. As expected, light footfalls could be heard entering the grotto from the far side. In the moonlight, the small silhouette of her frame, with the horizontal pole across its shoulders, could be seen. With silent, unspoken coordination, they sprang from their hiding spots amongst the rocks. Their fists were clenched and ready to cause injury. Unfortunately for them, they had neglected to bring any weapons.

Faster than they could comprehend, the shadowy

figure sank into a crouch as the pole swung through the air in a lightning-fast arc. It struck the first two boys across their shins, causing shrieks of pain to escape from their mouths. In less than a second, it was reconfigured and brought down hard on the shoulder of a third boy who was approaching. It was immediately brought back and thrust like a spear into the abdomen of a boy who was sneaking up from the rear. He doubled over and moaned as the wind was knocked out of him.

The last boy halted in place as the pole made another whip-like sweep through the air, narrowly missing the bridge of his nose. He held his hands up in a standard combat pose but thought twice before attacking. In the spectral light, his face met hers. She was crouched with most of her weight on her right leg, splayed and bent low to the ground. Her left leg was pointed ahead at a shallow angle with her foot extended lightly on the ground. She held the pole at an angle just above her right shoulder in a classic strike position. Even in his agitated state, he admired the perfection of her form. Her eyes, however, were apathetic, calculating and devoid of fear. This unnerved him. His felt himself becoming fidgety. Growing up with tales of leopards in the night and disappearing children, he was secretly uncomfortable here in the dark woods.

She, on the other hand, remained perfectly still, focused on him and placidly content that the others were incapacitated. After several moments, his pride finally yielded and he lowered his hands. She slowly stood and retreated out of the grotto toward the well. He could hear the unmistakable sound of full buckets being loaded onto a pole and then balanced onto a pair of shoulders. The remaining boy thought to himself in amazement, *She had already removed the buckets. How had she known?*

Now, on this day, she stood in the training room of the temple facing her mentor. Although no one, including herself, was aware of it, today was her seventeenth birthday. She was prepared mentally and physically for another challenge, another test of her endurance, strength, fortitude or resourcefulness. Little did she know, this next challenge would be well beyond her skill level or experience. He spoke.

58

"Helly, you will be leaving the monastery." In expected fashion, his words were concise and without feeling.

She wondered to herself, *For how long? For what purpose?*, but voiced nothing. She nodded once and continued giving her full attention to this man who had done his part to raise her. He continued. "You are going to the West."

To the west? As in the mountains to the west? Mentally, she began preparing a route and list of useful items if afforded. She nodded that she understood, but he knew she did not. In a rare moment, he broke from his formality and dropped his head slightly. He moved a step closer and spoke in a lower voice. "You are going to America."

Time froze. For the first time in...she couldn't remember, she was at a loss. A loss of words, a loss of a plan, a loss of control. Her heart rate accelerated without her permission. Her mouth dropped open slightly as her eyes searched left and right for some source of sense for what she was hearing. All of her life, talk of the Western culture had always been contextualized as the opposite of what should be pursued. America, in particular, had been used to contrast their way of life and, in her mind, was the epicenter of hedonism. *Why would I ever go to America? The people there are spoiled, lazy, violent, and selfish. Is this a test? My home is here.*

She did not have to ask why. Reading her thoughts, he began to explain. It would be the most words he would ever speak to her in one sitting. "There is one reason and there are a thousand. You are from America and it is likely you have family there as well. When we found you, we doubted that our government would exert any effort to locate them or return you there. To spare you from a short existence elsewhere, we decided to raise you as we would a boy who had been dedicated to us. But you are becoming more different from them with each passing day. You have been an object of scorn but will soon become an object of desire to them. It is the way of men and women."

All of these thoughts that had been exiled into the recesses of her mind were suddenly unleashed. She was suddenly extremely self-conscious and felt like hiding. *What is happening to me?*

He continued. "You need to experience the West. Isolation and hiding are two separate concepts. If their ways are more pleasing to you, we will let you choose. But to not know your options deprives you of any choice." This circular reasoning was suddenly very confusing. In the sterile environment of the temple, there was black and white, right and wrong, good and evil. But the playing field had just been enlarged exponentially. Gone was the constancy and familiarity this place had always offered. *Going to America?*

He drew closer and spoke even more tenderly. It filled her with possibly her first taste of anxiety. "You have to see for yourself. You have to try and locate any family you may have."

The possibility of this had always loomed silently on the sidelines of her thoughts, but it had now stepped directly in front of her life's path and refused to step aside. She felt, and then saw, the other monks slowly and reverently entering the room. Their proverbial solemn demeanors were now replaced with something more vulnerable. Their appearance caused her pulse to quicken once again. *This is really happening.*

They drew close and formed a semi-circle around her. Their expressions were unusually morose. It was as if they were actors participating in a theatrical play and she was the protagonist. She felt her throat tighten as her eyes became moist. The effect was contagious as several of the men fought back tears of their own. The bond between fathers and daughters transcends even the most disciplined of mindsets. They wanted to hold her, weep over her and die in the fight to protect her from the world, but centuries of dignity limited their affection to this melancholy gathering. She had been a gift from the heavens. She had been their little girl.

ALMOST THREE MONTHS AGO ZHENGZHOU XINZHENG INTERNATIONAL AIRPORT

The modern clothes felt simultaneously restrictive and revealing. She turned in front of the mirror and saw herself for the first time as the world would see her. The lady's public restroom had been an exercise in observation and imitation. She saw the other ladies go into the small cubicles, exit a few minutes later and then wash their hands at the row of sinks. That was completely understandable. What was not was the painting on their faces that they fastidiously tended to. They gently touched and adjusted large eyelashes and blood red lips. It reminded her of the shogun's face mask she'd seen in her history books. But these ladies did not appear to be outfitted for battle with their angled and pointy shoes and light, flowy shirts. No one paid her any notice, which she deeply appreciated.

Like a pinball, she bounced from tourist to tourist until she came to rest at her gate. She held the printed boarding pass and noticed that all of the other travelers had small tablets of various designs. As the herd began to migrate toward the door, each placed their tablet on a metallic pedestal and was rewarded with a pleasant audible tone. Then they passed through the door into a tunnel. Automatically, her eyes scanned the area for anything she could use as an improvised weapon. She was funneled along with the human current and ended up in an oddly round room. Another decorated lady guided her to an unusual chair that was thick with cushioning. She saw others place a belt across their laps, which she once again imitated. But the sensation that followed left her as queasy and uncomfortable as a seasick cat.

Everyone else seemed totally oblivious to the banshee-like wailing outside of the vehicle and the wild tilting of their seats. The world she had known fell away beneath the airplane. She gripped the armrests so that the veins in her forearms stood out from exertion. The other travelers continued to look at their small tablets, which changed in appearance by the moment. Others looked at flimsy books that were mostly pictures of highly decorated female warriors whose clothing would not do well in warfare.

She began to still herself as she closed her eyes and took an inventory of her sensations. She felt herself being gently pinned to the seat, the cool breeze coming from a small hole overhead and the smell of various flowers and musk around her. Slowly, she relaxed her grip and let her heart rate slow to something close to normal. For the next thirteen and a half hours, she developed mental images and expectations for what this adventure would hold. As the weeks ahead would prove, her imagination failed spectacularly.

John Cleveland

PART II

John Cleveland

Two Months Ago
Late Afternoon, 2095 Creston Ave, Richfield

The reflected face conveyed only approval. *Strong jaw, deep mysterious eyes, the slightest stubble, a conservative yet stylish hairstyle.* Then the face spoke. "Who's the one that the ladies like? Cody. Who's the strongest guy on our street? Cody is. Who has that magnetic appeal that makes others want to be around you? Cody does."

The reflected face gave a practiced smile, turning ever so slightly to the left and topped off the pose with a quick wink of the right eye. On this side of the mirror, Cody Ringwold was performing a final check before leaving to pick up his date. A magazine lay open on his bed, which was still unmade from the night before. An article in the Art of Masculinity had reported that pep talks before dates can increase testosterone levels by up to 22% and activate dormant pheromones. That, plus a spritz of Rodeo King cologne, were all intended to give him success tonight. He turned sideways and sucked in his gut as he admired his full profile. *Oh yeah. She is going to melt at the sight of you.*

The pheromone article obviously said nothing about humility.

John Cleveland

Meanwhile, at Samantha's Home, Simmons Lane, Richfield

Samantha, too, was looking in the mirror and hating what she saw. Anyone else would have described her as pretty, or even attractive. Her problem was that she was a late bloomer. She had been taller than the other girls, scrawny and gangly. She'd been the last one in her class to develop any shape and it didn't feel like she was catching up. Her perceived physical deficiencies, coupled with a laundry list of internal insecurities, all conspired to annihilate her self-esteem and confidence. Her stomach was a gnawing pit of anxiety. She thought she might actually vomit.

It's just a date. You don't have to marry him. But what if you never get married? What if this whole thing is a cruel prank and he's planning to publicly embarrass you? What if this is some elaborate form of cyber-bullying? What if you can't show your face at school on Monday? What if they start the same rumor that made Ramona have to transfer schools?

Of course, her name didn't rhyme with an epidemic virus. Still, she felt nauseous. Crippling anxiety seemed to plague most of the kids at her school. An ever-present sense of foreboding seemed to be piped in through the air vents. Samantha knew she was one of countless sufferers, but it did nothing to assuage her unease this evening.

Her therapist, at least the latest one, had given her a

written checklist to go through when she felt those feelings starting to surface. She looked down at the list:

#1. Smile. Obediently, she smiled at her reflection. It did make the opposing image more welcoming. It felt like she had climbed a single step upward out of her pit of despair.

#2. Positive Affirmation. She thought for a moment and tried to come up with a new line to feed herself. She locked eyes with the twin in the mirror and offered, "You are very good at algebra." For some reason, this statement caused her to slide two steps back. Not many guys are attracted to math skills.

#3. Declare Success for Future Goals. Again, she concentrated and tried to transmit confidence through the mirror and back to herself. "You are going to be fun and attractive tonight. He's going to tell everyone how wonderful you are and you will become so popular." Neither she nor the girl in the mirror was convinced.

She abandoned the list, noticed again all of her perceived flaws and slouched into utter disappointment. Looking at the mirror, she began to complain. "This is supposed to be fun. Why can't you just stop your crazy thoughts and enjoy yourself?" She almost swore that the reflected image wrinkled its upper lip and helplessly shrugged its shoulders.

He said goodbye to his mom and hopped in her minivan. As was his ritual, he leaned the seat back a few clicks, rolled down the windows, turned up the radio and put on his shades. He really should be driving a Mustang but, according to his calculations, it would require about 750 part time shifts at his current job. Sav-U-Lots was fine for the time being, but he doubted that it would be his final career choice. Of course, that estimate of time did not deduct for superfluous things like clothes, eating or taxes.

He slumped left toward the b-pillar of the door and gave a quick upward head nod to the girl stopped beside him at the red light. As the light turned green, she quickly pulled away without acknowledging the gesture. Plus, her Lexus had better acceleration than his mom's Kia.

Cody would not admit, and did not even realize, that his exaggerated machismo was actually his way of compensating for insecurity. Although he'd spent time with girls at camp, this was his first official date. It would be the first time he'd not needed a ride from his mom, had not needed to borrow money from his mom, and (if everything went well) would receive a kiss from somebody other than his mom. Underneath the Elvis-like smirk and flared out arms of intimidation, he was intimidated. Any time the nervous feelings began to smolder, he quickly doused them with another self-affirmation.

Upon arriving at the address, he checked his teeth in the rearview mirror and cupped his hand over his mouth to check his breath. Satisfied that he was ready, he winked at the reflected eyes and imagined the honor that his awaiting date felt at being chosen. Thankfully, he eased off of the machismo long enough to be polite to her mom as she let him in through the front door. They were still at an age when parents could easily and immediately shut down a budding romance.

He opened the passenger door to the minivan for her and then waved to the mom, who was watching from the porch. He was pretty sure she snapped a photo with her phone. *Just great. I'm sure everyone on Facebook is going to see me...without my Mustang.*

Like most teenagers, the conversation was stilted and awkward. Too many mental pressures were bouncing through their thoughts to discuss anything of substance. *Are we going to hold hands? Do I smell OK? Are we going to kiss? What about my breath? Are they dating anybody else? Could I see myself being married to this person?* Crazy thoughts that are very premature and ruinous to a good evening. So, they cruised inelegantly toward The Feeding Trough in the Kia minivan, her freshly curled hair tangling hopelessly in the windy, open cabin.

She had valid concerns for her hair but was too nervous to voice them. *I worked so hard to curl it and set it but now it's blowing all over the place! Why does he have the windows down? Doesn't the A/C work?* Cody just remained tilted against the door, head bobbing to the way-too-loud music that threatened to blow the factory speakers. *Is this really what I should expect from dating? From guys? Why am I so worked up over all of this?*

Her mind imagined a hypothetical scene five years in the future. They are married. She's pregnant with their second child and burning up in the passenger seat. Their infant is crying inconsolably in his car seat, but his father just turns up the volume to drown it all out. For some reason, they are still in his mom's minivan. She involuntarily shuddered as her mind returned to the present.

Meanwhile, he continued to stoke his own ego. *The coolest music, the coolest moves, not talking much to remain mysterious. I bet she's dreaming of us being together*. Nightmares are technically dreams, so his assessment of the situation was oddly accurate.

Mingled with the same thoughts of self-flattery were more critical reflections. *She alright, I guess. Nothing exotic. A tan and some muscle tone would probably boost her from a 7 to a 9*. In his mind, he deserved a 9. After all, he was pretty high on the spectrum himself. And joining the gym, coupled with his new Rodeo King cologne, were just icing on an already sweet cake. *Beefcake, that is*. He nodded and smiled at his own joke.

The little minivan turned into The Feeding Trough which advertised "Friday night – Fried Chicken, All-U-Can Eat $9.99." His mouth began to water.

One Month Ago
Behind 303 Raven Lane, Richfield

The windows of the tiny and dilapidated camper trailer flickered as it sat in the backyard of a house that was in an equal state of disrepair. An orange extension cord and green hosepipe were connected to its rippled aluminum exterior. Its use as a rental property probably violated a dozen city ordinances, but the landlord liked earning an extra $400 a month from something that he'd considered towing away to the dump. Little did he know (or care), the trailer's occupant was unable to pay the rent without some creative (and illegal) ways of procuring income.

It's not fair, Dustin Marlow thought to himself angrily. His face was contorted into a snarl as he watched a mindless TV show on his flat screen with a blur in the top left corner. It had been damaged during the move into this dump. No big deal. He'd only paid $15 dollars for it at a yard sale. But it was not the poor image quality that was fueling his ire.

It was the gorgeous girl sitting on the couch next to the handsome bachelor. She was one of twelve girls competing for his affection on the latest reality show, "The Catch." She, like all the others, was amazingly attractive, fit and completely smitten with this one guy. *What's so special about him anyway? So what if he invented the Accolades App? I mean, who needs a smartphone to come up with a compliment for your date? It's not fair.* He continued to fume as the wealthy bachelor casually sorted through the girls as if he were picking out which shirt to wear for the day.

He began to ponder ways that he could have a woman like that. He racked his brain for almost ten minutes trying to come up with an idea for an app, but he knew absolutely nothing about developing technology. Lottery? No money for tickets. Bank robbery? No gun. No mask. No getaway car. Mail order bride? Once again, no money. Option after option was stamped as "rejected," which further intensified his frustration.

He thought about the beauties down at the beach, or even at the park. He had seen a cartoon once where a caveman was lonely, so he grabbed his club and left his rock den in search of a mate. When he stumbled upon a woman, he bonked her on the head and dragged her back to his lair by her ankle. It was likely produced in an era when barbaric humor wasn't taken seriously, but at the end of the day, the caveman had his woman. Once she came to, she quickly became accustomed to her new home and her man. His mind used this fantasy to contemplate this as an option. But it was also rejected. No time machine.

One Month Ago
Samantha's Home,
Simmons Lane, Richfield

"What do you mean that I'm lucky to be going out with you?" Samantha held the phone against her right ear and held her left hand against her forehead. She sat on the edge of her bed and felt like she was sliding down into a chasm with no way back out. She had been dating Cody for a month now and he'd quickly become manically possessive. In one breath, he'd be talking about how it needed to be just the two of them, all the time. The next moment, he'd be talking about all the girls he could be going out with. He had lost his mind and she was losing hers.

There were more words from his end of the conversation. She exhaled with exasperation and replied, "I do like you, but I don't know about love. That feels like it should be reserved for something serious." Apparently, that didn't land well because loud words could be heard from the earpiece, half screaming, half crying. His emotions were so volatile. He'd act so tough and cool and then fall apart like a Jenga tower without warning. Then he'd tell her that she was everything to him and beg her not to talk to anyone else.

She, like most girls, wanted to be loved and adored, but why did it have to be so tumultuous? Why couldn't it be sweet and peaceful? She could envision a future with him being like this but even more volatile. However, the alternative of being alone was equally terrifying. What if no one else wanted her? What if he really was the best she could do?

Maybe he was right.

One Month Ago
Greater Metropolis of Richfield

Two weeks in the United States and she would sleep under a roof for the first time tonight. As Helly's mentors had explained, the United States would initially be a whirlwind of input and stimulation, audibly, visually and emotionally. She had been instructed to leave the airport and to walk without stopping to the nearest forest she could find. This may have seemed severe to an outsider, but there was a method to their madness. One of her mentors, the English teacher, had been to the United States so he had special insight to offer her. He, along with the others, felt that it would be best for her to intentionally distance herself and then to slowly acclimate to the culture.

In the walk from the terminal, she focused on where she would be walking and purposefully avoided eye contact with anyone or anything. The lights, the noise, the scents all fought to overwhelm her usually serene senses. Even in her peripheral vision, it all felt like static to her nerves. Hours went by, block after endless block, but eventually she was in the midst of trees. Like open arms, she felt welcomed by their branches as they muffled out the chaos of where she had been. It was an easy chore to find a secluded and safe spot, erect a lean-to and prepare a mattress out of spruce boughs. The higher elevation was a nice respite from the city heat and a brook was located not too far away to quench her thirst.

That first night, she had gone to the edge of the woods, climbed a tree and looked out over the city. The sea of lights was mesmerizing. Red rivers of taillights flowed through the canyons of buildings like colored canals of water. She'd never been so close to so much infrastructure or so many people. A blend of leeriness and curiosity encompassed her mind. After all, these were Westerners: materialistic, lazy, hedonistic, selfish, volatile.

On the other hand, she was genetically one of them. How could she look upon them with any judgment? Perhaps everyone is a product of their environment. Had she been fortunate to be raised by the Shaolin? Had she been deprived of some great joy that these Westerners knew? And what of her future? These questions extended to the horizons of her thoughts and suddenly felt very burdensome. She had been warned that this would happen, an inundation of stimuli and unwanted thoughts. Before things spun out of control, she closed her eyes and took an inventory of her senses. She felt the bark of the limb on which she was perched, inhaled the pine aromas and listened to the distant, low roar of traffic. After several long moments, she opened her eyes and developed a plan, a strategy if you will, on how to discover this new world.

She was still curious as to how the monks had purchased her plane ticket, bought her modern clothes and given her $1,200 cash. However it had been accomplished, she understood that it had required great sacrifice. She thought about some ancient heirloom of the temple that had possibly been exchanged for her departure fare. She thought about the fourteen years that they had altered their way of life, concession after concession, so that she might live and be who she is today. But who is that? She had no friends, no family, no home, no income. Reverting back to her training, she did not perceive these as deficiencies or injustices. Instead, they were obstacles that would cause growth of strength in her mind and body. They were to be analyzed, attacked and appreciated. Lodging would be her first goal.

Each day, she ventured into the edges of the city. Every street had a name and every house had a number. She noticed that people outside of their homes would sometimes wave, quickly lift their chin or even speak to acknowledge her. It provided a great sense of inclusion to return these gestures. She was certain that her mannerisms and pronunciation must have been peculiar to these Westerners, but she had yet to be singled out as a foreigner. Once again, she reminded herself that by appearances, she blended in perfectly.

As she observed other girls her age, she noticed behavioral extremes. Some were socially reclusive with their heads lowered. Speech and eye contact were virtually nonexistent. Others were brazen and flaunted their feminine attributes as if they were performing. Like the ladies in the airport restroom, they too had brightly painted faces, but their clothing was much more revealing. Helly felt embarrassed even though she was properly covered. She concluded that either alternative was birthed from insecurity. Had these young ladies realized their true worth, the extremes of seclusion or flamboyance could be avoided. Her more refined conduct was the end result of nearly perfected humility and respect.

The boys were even more perplexing. They typically walked in groups and would focus their attention on her without extending any type of greeting. It seemed like they were evaluating her and continued to do so even after she had passed by. Without actually looking, she could somehow perceive that they were craning their necks to evaluate her from behind until she was out of sight. Were the males here responsible for governing young ladies? Was she in violation of some law or custom? She gained insight into this mysterious relationship between genders the following day.

As she was walking down the sidewalk, a group of three guys approached directly ahead. The one in the center noticed her and elbowed both of his friends to gain their attention. Each began to grin as they drew near. The middle one spoke.

"Hey, Boo. I haven't seen you around here before. What's your name?"

She saw no reason not to answer. Robotically, she stated, "My name is Helly."

"Helly. That's a pretty name. I'm Mike and these are my boys, Dillan and Slate." She bowed slightly before she realized that people did not do that here. Quickly, she tried to recall some American phrases that she had been taught.

"You are all very far out," she offered.

Puzzled faces met her neutral expression.

She tried again, "I mean that you are all really happening."

The middle guy raised an eyebrow and asked, "Are you high?"

She was not sure of the context, so she decided to cut this conversation short. "Well, keep on truckin'." She quickly skirted them to the left and continued walking down the sidewalk. She could feel their eyes on her backside and suddenly felt exposed.

One called out, "Hey, crazy. You fill those jeans out nice!"

Her face flushed and felt warm as she realized they were verbalizing lustful thoughts. This was strictly forbidden in the monastery. To even allow the thoughts was detrimental, but entertaining them or expressing them was beyond her comprehension. She felt her fists clench as she spun around and crouched.

Their eyes went wide and their mouths fell open. The middle one let out an expletive. The one to his left tapped him on the chest and said, "Come on, dude. This one is really psycho." They shook their heads and muttered as they turned to go on their way.

She slowly stood and relaxed her hands as she tried to decipher this strange encounter. She made a mental list of things learned. Apparently, it was socially acceptable to speak with men in public. However, they were primarily interested only in physical gratification. They had not been threatening, just rude and juvenile. Combat readiness was not a normal reaction. And lastly, her English teacher was not current on his street talk.

She had explored the immediate area and discovered that a barracks of sorts existed where one could pay a small fee to stay overnight. It was called The Hiker's Hostel. With everything she owned stored in her backpack, she paid for one night to learn what lodging in America was like.

She had seen a similar toilet in the American airport so that mystery was quickly solved. The shower, however, was a new experience. By sheer chance, she turned the valve marked H and stepped into the stream. The cold water seemed completely normal, but the pressurized nozzle was a new experience. *This should make washing more effective,* she thought. But within seconds, the water became warm, and then hot, and then scalding. She was trained to tolerate physical extremes, but this was madness.

She leapt through the plastic curtain and warily eyed the torturous torrent. *From what I've been told, Americans are not well equipped for enduring such pain.* With that in mind, she investigated the valve marked C and turned it. The water began to cool to something like pond water. She tentatively reentered the stream and thought how pleasant it was not to be freezing. She suspected that warm but not scalding water was possible, so she continued to adjust the mixture until something like paradise began to flow from the shower head. It was pure bliss. And there seemed to be no end to it.

The water continued to flow for minute after luxurious minute. She was truly caught up in the experience when she thought about the American's insatiable quest for comfort. With sudden and forced determination, she cut off the water and exited the shower. *I will not be lured into a life of ease and laziness.* But the desire had been embedded.

Three Weeks Ago
Maple Ridge Greenway

Dustin first saw her near the fountain. He thought it was odd that she drank from the pool even though she did not look homeless. Her clothes were neat and clean, her hair was smooth and she looked healthy. Very healthy. And excitement grew in the pit of his stomach. Plus, she was small. He liked that.

He had not come out of the womb with aspirations of being evil. In his mind, none of the things he did were actually wrong. If he was fortunate enough to find a purse unattended, its owner should have kept a closer watch on it. If copper or aluminum scrap was lying around, he felt that taking it to the junkyard was actually recycling (which was good for the earth). If a few fences or padlocks needed to be circumvented, he justified it by his "love for the planet." If his hunger was greater than his desire to work, Buckston's Grocery could absorb the cost of some stolen merchandise. All companies factored in a certain percentage of loss when they reconciled their books.

In his defense, Dustin had never been exposed to a good example of anything. Growing up in a hostile and filthy environment, he was only cognizant of a "better way" through the lens of envy. The people that lived in better houses, drove better cars and had better women were, in essence, cheaters. They had found a way to escape or avoid the hopeless pit of poverty that he'd been born into. He thought endlessly about how to use theft, deceit or even force to follow in their footsteps. Seldom if ever was hard work considered.

As for Dustin's ideas about the opposite sex, they were formed in part by the example of his parents, but mostly by television. In his mind, a woman's first priority should be to become as attractive as possible and then to maintain that level of desirability for as long as possible. Her second should be to please her man, which included serving or being available for whatever his needs were. His mom had failed miserably in both of these "responsibilities," which in some sick way justified the abuse that his father dished out both verbally and physically.

Returning his focus to the fountain, he continued to evaluate his newest item of interest.

She looked lost or naïve, or maybe innocent was more accurate. She appeared to be watching the people around her and, at times, seemed to be replicating and practicing some of the gestures and exchanges taking place around her. She acted like a confused tourist but did not look like one. *Easy target,* he said to himself.

The water was foul. It had a strange, unnatural taste mixed with duck droppings. As she wiped her mouth, she happened to see a small child nearby receiving help from their mother to drink from a small concrete pedestal. She walked over and asked the lady, "How much does it cost to drink from the fountain?"

The lady looked a little perplexed, but smiled and

answered. "It's free. It's a public water fountain."

She looked at the apparatus and deduced that the small, metal button would cause the water to flow. She pressed it, which caused a small stream to arch over the little bowl. Hesitantly, she leaned over and licked the stream of water like a dog. She heard laughter and turned to see the lady covering her mouth. "I'm sorry. I don't mean to laugh. Are you visiting the United States?"

Helly knew that attempting to deceive this lady would be futile. "Yes. I am."

"Where from?" She was sincere and warm.

"I am from China, the Henan Province."

"Wow! But...you look completely American. I'm sorry. I know we're not supposed to talk about where people were born or how they look."

"This is rude to do so?"

"Oh, dear. You really are not from here. Let's just say that people have become very sensitive about a lot of things." She extended her hand and smiled.

Helly replicated the gesture and allowed her hand to be shaken lightly. It felt nice.

"My name is Helly."

"Well, hello, Helly. That's a beautiful name. I'm Mandy and this is my daughter, Maddie." The little girl blubbered something unintelligible but waved open palmed toward Helly. She also replicated this gesture.

A thought exploded in her mind. *This is what most girls grow up with. A mother.* Some faint image of a beautiful, brown haired young woman smiling down at her appeared in her mind. It felt like a memory but it was so vague. Just being in the presence of this woman caused her to want to smile.

"You are a mother," she stated.

"Yes, I am. For almost two years now. Do you have family in town?"

"I do not know. It is possible."

Mandy suddenly looked concerned. "I don't mean to pry, but are you staying with someone? Are you safe?"

"I am safe and I have stayed at the hostel."

"With the hikers? You don't look like a hiker."

Helly wasn't sure what a hiker was or was supposed to look like.

"It is within my budget and has facilities for washing."

Mandy's brow furrowed further and Helly realized that she was being evaluated again; however, it did not feel the same as when the young men had appraised her. For some reason, she enjoyed the woman's concern. The woman was obviously contemplating something.

Mandy had always had a soft heart for the helpless. How many injured birds and orphaned squirrels had she brought home to her own mother during her childhood? She would share her lunch with a fellow student who she knew came from a poor family. Her parents soon learned to give her just a few modest gifts for Christmas because they would likely be distributed to strangers that she thought needed them more than she did. She was just naturally kind. It was in her, like a strand of DNA that rarely occurs in humans. The downside of this blind benevolence is that her family members inevitably had to share in the consequences, good or bad. She was about to commit another hasty act of altruism, and the wisdom of it would only be measured in the weeks to come.

"Would you consider staying in our garage apartment, just for tonight? I don't like the thought of you sleeping out there all alone."

Helly was not sure if she meant the woods or the hostel. The monks had told her that she would have to rely not only on her training but also her intuition. She knew that she would eventually have to accept the kindness of strangers and establish relationships. With no indication of any threat, she decided to accept the lady's offer.

"Yes. Thank you. That would be groovy."

Simmons Lane, Richfield

As they walked down the sidewalk toward her home, Mandy continued to gently interview this mysterious stranger. "So, Helly. How long will you be here?"

"I do not have a definitive time schedule. I was sent here to seek out a connection with the people from whom I originated."

Mandy's face accurately reflected her puzzled reaction to that answer. "I'm sorry, honey. I don't think I've ever met someone your age, or anyone for that matter, who speaks so articulately. You must have had an amazing English teacher."

Helly's mind drifted half a world away to the monks who had served as surrogate fathers to her. She felt a sudden ache of homesickness in her heart. "Yes. He was an excellent teacher. However, I am beginning to wonder if his knowledge of idioms has become obsolete."

Mandy laughed again. "That explains the *groovy*. I don't think people have said that since Woodstock."

"Woodstock?" Helly asked.

"It was a big music festival back in the 1960s. Everyone was protesting the war and doing drugs and wearing bell-bottoms. Those have come back in style the last few years, but the slang has not."

"Bell-bottoms?"

Mandy displayed a natural patience as she explained. "They were a type of blue jeans where the bottom portions had tons of fabric. It looked like you were wearing big bells around your ankles."

"Did this make one more effective in combat or provide some type of protection?"

Mandy's left eyebrow raised at the mention of combat. "Um, no. The people that tended to wear them were strongly opposed to combat."

Helly continued to process and ponder the non-sensical ways that apparently permeated Western culture.

The Masons' Home,
Simmons Lane, Richfield

Mandy unlocked the door on the side of her garage and turned on the light switch. She noticed that Helly cautiously entered and swept her eyes over the contents of the building. They moved up the stairs to the built-in attic where Mandy opened the door to an A-framed room. It contained a single bed, a nightstand with a lamp and a set of wooden shelves.

"We built this in for my parents. They try to visit as often as they can while Maddie is still little. They just flew home last Friday. I've already put fresh sheets on the bed and clean towels in the bathroom. You should have everything you need. I'll introduce you to my husband when he gets home from work this afternoon. I'll give you some time to freshen up and rest while I go put Maddie down for a nap. Make yourself at home!" With a warm smile, she turned and shut the door on her way out.

Helly examined the bed with its ultra plush mattress and assortment of almost a dozen small pillows. *How many people sleep in such a small bed?* She then investigated the bathroom, which was spotless with a pleasant scent of flowers. It had the same amenities as the one she had used in the hostel, but this one did not appear to be used by many. She pondered the possibility that this one was to be exclusively used by the occupants of this room. *Such affluence.*

She then moved toward the shelves, which had a collection of books and what she would later learn to be knickknacks. There were framed photos of Mandy with a smaller version of Maddie and a handsome man who was close to Mandy's age. They were standing on a street lined with very colorful buildings. It ended at an amazingly ornate castle complete with parapets and towers. There were people dressed as large, clothed animals and everyone seemed to be accompanied by small children. In her geography lessons, she had never been told about this strange and fascinating nation. Apparently, it was the custom of guests to wear small black hats with round circles protruding from their tops. Helly would never insult Mandy by saying it aloud, but she thought it gave them the appearance of mice.

John Cleveland

Samantha's Home,
Simmon's Lane, Richfield

Samantha had been looking across the street as Mandy returned home with the teenage girl. She watched with curiosity as they disappeared into their garage. *Who is that girl? A niece?* She felt an unsettling blend of emotions in her gut. Any variation in her day caused a small sense of dread as her mind fabricated various possibilities of disaster. *Mandy will start ignoring you. You've been replaced. She's probably mean. That girl probably has a ton of boyfriends that she'll flaunt as she goes out on dates. She's probably going to start posting rumors about you on social media.* On and on, her mind fueled the acidic response of her stomach. However, a single thought pierced the sea of dark thoughts. *Maybe she's nice.*

2095 Creston Ave, Richfield

Cody was lying on his bed. The latest song by Below the Belt was blaring from his stereo. He was lazily curling a five-pound dumbbell with his left arm and holding the latest issue of the Art of Masculinity magazine in his right hand. The article of interest was entitled "Body Odor - Deterrent or Desire Magnet?" He subconsciously angled his nose toward his left armpit and took a sniff. It wasn't very appealing to him, but who was he to question the professionals? In his mind, their entire magazine staff consisted of highly acclaimed scientists and relationship experts whose research carried the same credibility as the Encyclopedia Brittanica.

At the predictable six second increment, he thought about girls for the millionth time. Samantha is OK, for now. She's a safe bet and good to keep in my pocket. She's probably writing her first name and your last name in a notebook over and over again, dreaming of the day we walk down the aisle. But do I even want to get married? After all, it would be a crime to deny so many ladies the chance to go out with a highly eligible bachelor like me. His teenage mind was incapable of realizing that "highly eligible" was a kind way of indicating "low demand."

But is Samantha exotic? Cody pondered this seriously and began to visualize himself walking on some beach in Hawaii with a deeply tanned girl who was wearing a grass skirt and flower lei. For some reason, in this fantasy she spoke no English, but was irresistibly drawn to him even without the benefit of conversation. She leaned into him and inhaled his natural aroma. The corners of his mouth lifted into a grin as he increased the intensity of his curling. At least his left arm would be impressive.

The Mason's Home,
Simmons Lane, Richfield

That was a real dirtbag move. Tom Mason turned his Honda Odyssey minivan into their neighborhood after a challenging day at work. Mentally, he was on cruise control as he absentmindedly navigated through the familiar streets. His mind was still back in the office where co-workers knifed you in the back. *I can't believe they gave the Holly-Ham account to Jeremy. Wait! They didn't give it to him. He practically stole it. Jerk.*

He was stewing over what he considered to be an injustice. After majoring in marketing, he landed a job at a small advertising firm in Bankston, a larger town about twenty-five minutes away (barring bad traffic). At times, it felt like his career was slowly gaining traction and building momentum. However, days like today made him feel like a board game piece sliding all the way back to start on Chutes and Ladders.

Maybe I should play dirty like the other guys: fudge the truth, make promises you know you can't fulfill, schmooze the boss. He knew he never actually would, but the temptation to do so crept up without fail. His sour expression accurately reflected his attitude as he turned onto their street.

A visible transformation suddenly came over him. *Something* interrupted his thoughts which, in turn, changed his countenance.

My girls. A coy grin crept across his face as their faces materialized in his mind. He was in love - times two. The shift was about to occur. As the minivan turned onto the concrete driveway of their suburban sanctuary and came to a stop, he moved the gearshift lever into park and his mind into "dad mode." The frustrations of the day would not corrupt his family time. He would not allow it to.

In memories of his own childhood, he thought of his father, who had always managed to keep things in balance. He thought back to a time when his dad had been offered an impressive promotion that would have revolutionized their financial status. But Tom's dreams of a swimming pool and an in-home theater disappeared in a puff of smoke when his dad came home and told the family that he was going to remain in his current position. Perceiving his disappointment, he asked Tom if he'd like to share his thoughts. Tom, still young and immature, was pouting as he scornfully answered, "I just wanted our neighbors to be impressed by us." In his mind, this seemed like a laudable goal.

He remembered his dad reflecting on the sentiment before he answered. "Tom, you're only going to be young once. If I had taken that promotion, I would be traveling almost every week. I'm choosing my family. I'm choosing the memories I'll have in the future instead of the money." It took some time for a young Tom to realize that his dad was right, but thinking back to all of the experiences they had together, he now felt immense gratitude that his father had put his family first.

Tom looked into his own eyes staring back in the

rearview mirror. "Have you gotten it out of your system?" he asked aloud. "Need to whine or complain anymore before we go inside?" The reflected eyes flashed an indignant repulsion and then relaxed as "Work Tom" became "Daddy Tom." It was easy to do. His devotion to Mandy was effortless. It had not taken much time in the world of matrimony to realize that what he enjoyed at home was much different from the relationships of his co-workers. Whereas they constantly complained about their wives' continual nagging, incessant spending and laziness, he generally had warm thoughts about his.

Aside from being a natural beauty, with or without makeup, she was good to him: complimentary, appreciative, supportive. Like any marriage, some days were better than others, but their five years together had contained a ton of smiles and an equal measure of laughter. As newlyweds, she had worked hard at her job, doing her best to help establish them financially. When the home pregnancy test told them they were going to be parents, they had already decided that she would stay at home. It seemed reasonable to both of them that if they were going to have a kid, they should be the ones to raise it. With this agreement in mind, he secretly vowed to himself that he would take on extra jobs, cut yards or even sell a kidney on the black market to provide for his family. So far, God had provided.

Shutting the Odyssey's door, he used his key to enter and slipped off his shoes in the mud room. It was a habit he was trying to develop because Mandy appreciated clean floors. He smiled knowing that a warm kiss from Mandy was waiting just beyond the kitchen door. Immediately after that, he would turn and scoop up the other love of his life. His feelings for Maddie did not compete with those he had for his wife but mysteriously complemented and completed them. Inhaling and exhaling once more, he paused to relish the nervous excitement growing in his gut. He opened the door.

The reward of their reception instantly erased the labors of his work day. After a prolonged peck on the lips, Mandy returned to the stove where a scrumptious scent was emanating from the collection of pots. Maddie dropped her toy in the living room and ran with arms outstretched and dimples from her smile in full effect. He scooped her up and lifted her high above his head before pulling her down to eye level and planting a barrage of noisy, silly kisses all over her face. She squealed with delight and a mysterious chemistry began to permeate his veins. *How can I love her this much?* This was totally different from the romantic feelings he shared with Mandy, but were every bit as strong. This emotion overshadowed everything in that moment and the only word that could describe his current state was blessed.

As he continued to bounce and bob with little Maddie in his arms, he made his way over to the stove to get a sneak peek at tonight's dinner. "Looks like a lot of food. You tryin' to fatten me up?" he joked.

Mandy paused as if carefully forming her next words. "Someone is actually joining us tonight." The silence that followed was odd. His face wrinkled to reflect his puzzlement. Mandy opened her mouth and paused again before blurting out, "I brought home a girl from the park today. She's actually in the garage."

His left eyebrow raised as he digested her news. His mind contemplated the possibilities. *Did she kidnap someone's child? No. That's crazy. Did she bring home a street person? Maybe. I could totally see her doing that. Can you be too compassionate? What about Maddie's safety?* His normal human thoughts continued to entertain him.

"I thought about calling you, but I didn't want to bother you at work and," Mandy's eyes searched the ceiling for a justification, "it just felt right."

He imagined an unwashed bag lady lying on the boutique bed they had worked so hard to decorate in their guest house. He pictured her getting up and leaving behind a dirty imprint in the shape of her body. He inwardly shuddered while feeling guilty about the demeaning thought. His heart thumped as someone knocked on the back door. He spun around and was surprised to see a clean, young face looking at him through the glass. *Is this her? Who is she? Is she a runaway? Should I call the police?* As his thoughts ran astray, he realized that he could not keep her outside while he discussed this with Mandy. Sometimes, marriage requires blind trust without an explanation. Although he would get better at this as the years passed, he would pass this evening's test with flying colors.

He walked over and opened the door to see a girl about seventeen years of age. Initially, she looked completely American, but Tom was astute. This girl wore no makeup and her demeanor was mature, oddly so. She made eye contact, bowed her head slightly and offered a very flat, "Hello. My name is Helly."

The events of the last sixty seconds had thrown him off balance and he found himself bowing with Maddie slumping forward clumsily in his arms. He shook his head and remembered to smile as he regained his composure. He stuck out his hand and warmly introduced himself. "Hi, Helly. I'm Tom. Come in!"

She slowly shook his hand with way too much formality and then walked inside to the kitchen. He watched as her eyes surveyed the room as if taking in each detail and formulating some kind of plan.

An odd uneasiness formed in his stomach as he snuck a look at Mandy. She shrugged helplessly and made an indiscernible gesture with her head after Helly's gaze passed by. She quickly shifted into "hospitable host" mode. "Hi, Helly! I set a place for you right beside Maddie's high chair. I hope your shirt isn't dry clean only!" She laughed alone at her joke as Helly stared back blankly. Mandy tried to clarify. "Maddie can be quite the mess maker." No response. Tom's smile appeared slightly forced as the evening he was expecting suddenly felt in jeopardy.

Helly stood behind the chair she identified as her own and remained in a position almost resembling the military's *attention.*

"Please, have a seat. Make yourself at home," Mandy continued.

Tom finally got it together and forced himself to loosen up. He jiggled Maddie's legs into the child seat and put a bib around her neck before taking a seat across the table. "So, Helly. How did you and Mandy meet?"

Helly began to recount their interaction at the park. "Your wife demonstrated how to use the drinking fountain and inquired about my background. She graciously extended the use of your home and expressed concern about my safety."

Tom nodded and tried to remain casual. "I see. Is there

a reason to be concerned about your safety? We'll be glad to call your family."

With the same absence of emotion, she countered, "I do not know if I have any family. My parents were killed when I was a small child, roughly the same age as your own." Helly nodded to Maddie sitting in the high chair to her left. Her words were devoid of emotion.

There was an awkward pause in the conversation until Tom finally said, "I'm so sorry. Were you raised in foster care? An orphanage?"

"I was raised in a monastery in China. They have been the only family I have known, but they have sent me here to America so that I can look for any, how do you say, bloody relatives?"

Tom flinched but was rescued by Mandy as she corrected, "I think you mean blood relatives. It means your sisters, brothers, parents, grandparents, cousins, people like that."

Tom was doing his best to decipher this bizarre situation his wife had created. The more cynical side of him was beginning to suspect that his girl was some type of robotic psycho that could, at any moment, grab a steak knife and murder everyone in the room. In the moment, he had no way of knowing that her mental stability exceeded even that of his own. Also, the fact that she was highly trained and physically capable of completing such an act was better left unknown.

Mandy brought two pots to the table and sat down. "Helly has been staying at the hostel over on Riverfront Avenue."

"Are you a hiker?" Tom asked.

"I have been camping for several days as a form of orientation. I was cautioned that the urban environment can be overstimulating and overwhelming."

Tom's wrinkled forehead and raised eyebrows continued to betray him. "Helly, would you excuse us for just a moment? I need to ask Mandy a question...in the other room."

Helly sat there almost motionless as they awkwardly left the table.

Once away from earshot, Mandy began the volley. "I know this is strange, Tom, but it just happened. I couldn't just leave her there. She was drinking out of the pond. The duck pond. I don't know what to make of her, but I feel like she needs help."

Tom was still trying to wrap his head around this. "Don't you think we should call the police? She could be a runaway or a crazy person. Do you hear how she talks?"

"She talks like a foreigner with good English. We talked all the way home. Everything lines up with her story. If it's true, we don't want to scare her. Poor thing. Can you imagine what she must be going through? How would you have done all alone in a foreign country at her age?"

Tom sighed and mentally weighed his options. "I appreciate you being concerned about strangers, but as the man of this house, I have to be concerned about you and Maddie." At the mention of her name, they both leaned so that they could lay eyes on their little girl in the next room.

Mandy continued, "Maybe we're making this weirder than it has to be. We're not doing anything wrong or illegal, so let's see where this goes. If she says anything off-the-wall, I'll sneak out and call the police."

With that, they returned to the table while forcing themselves to act normal. Mandy took over. "Helly, do you mind if we pray for the food?"

Helly looked puzzled. "I am familiar with prayer and its purpose but the animal that feeds us is beyond the benefit of prayer."

Mandy elaborated. "It's an expression. It just means that we are going to thank God for this meal."

Helly nodded and asked, "How do I participate in this custom?"

"Well, Tom will say the blessing, I mean prayer, and we just close our eyes and bow our heads."

Closing one's eyes in a new environment was contrary to her training, but she had already analyzed the room, identified items that could be improvised weapons and assessed the combat readiness of her hosts. She allowed herself to close her eyes, bow her head and observe only with her ears.

"Father, we thank you for this food. Thank you for the day you have given us and for this evening to rest and enjoy each other's company. Thank you especially for our new friend, Helly, and please show us how we can help her. In Your name we pray, Amen." Mandy repeated this final word and even Maddie offered some semblance of it. At this, everyone opened their eyes as serving spoons began to ladle out the various offerings.

Helly felt the edge of her alertness softening ever so slightly as questions began to bounce across the table. She watched with keen attention as this couple shared details about their day with an emphasis on the things Maddie had done. She contemplated that if circumstances had been different, she too would have probably grown up in a home similar to this and with parents like this. This would be considered normal. She couldn't know at this point that other homes and families did not experience this level of harmony. For the second time in her life, Helly had been delivered from an airplane into the caring arms of strangers.

The next morning, Helly woke up before sunrise, which was her custom and natural body rhythm. As her eyes popped open, they moved around the room to orient herself and remind her of her current surroundings. She reclosed her eyes and inhaled intentionally through her nose. After a pause of about four seconds, she slowly blew out through pursed lips until her abs tightened. She repeated this sequence three more times and then awkwardly slid off of the mattress into a crouching position. *What is the purpose of sleeping on so much cushioning?* she thought to herself as she evaluated the elevated box springs, mattress, topper and comforter. She agreed with herself that if she was allowed to sleep here again, she would prepare a bedroll on the floor. After all, one would opt to walk on firm ground as opposed to a swamp. Sleeping should also follow this natural preference.

From her crouching position, she transitioned to a kneeling position, where she continued her intentional breathing. With her eyes closed, she concentrated on the sensation of exchanging carbon dioxide for oxygen. As her mind cleared, she could feel, or at least sense, her pulse in her neck. She felt the plush carpet under the tops of her feet as well as the morning sunlight casting its warmth on her face through the windows. In the practice of mindfulness, a person is supposed to train their focus on the present sensations. Its purpose is to divert one's thoughts from injustices of the past or worries about the future by only thinking about the here and now.

Like other disciplines, Helly had perfected the ability to shift her thinking in order to quell any detrimental emotions. However, in the fringes of her consciousness, she pondered the mystery of how so many anatomical systems with such amazing sensitivities could have developed simultaneously. How could each work in conjunction with the others inside of a package that was mechanically amazing, efficient and relatively low maintenance? As a child, the answers to such questions were nebulous and avoided any concrete explanation. Instead of any factual description, the entire issue was skirted by saying that the universe had no origin but is in a continual process of rebirth.

Being a half-world away from her mentors had subconsciously granted her an unexpected liberty to investigate truths about life and existence. Questioning the traditional views had been discouraged up until now, but Helly felt strangely and suddenly capable of looking at the world and coming to her own conclusions. As she morphed her breathing into a regimen of controlled movements, she felt a novel stirring in her stomach. It was excitement. She was excited to see what the day held and to learn why life in America had been both demonized and desired by the rest of the world. She would remain leery but observant.

Behind 303 Raven Lane, Richfield

After waking up around 10:00 AM, Dustin stumbled into the grungy bathroom that was literally the size of a phone booth. The flimsy plastic walls were warped and cracked in various places. Old clothes hung from the showerhead and valves, which had not been used in months. Considering the low monthly rate of this "residence," you could not expect any maintenance or upkeep. After relieving himself in a mysteriously dry toilet, he turned toward the mirror.

He looked at the unkempt image and hated what he saw. Aside from the tousled hair and acne scattered face, he inwardly loathed what lurked behind those cold hazel eyes. He cursed his parents for their unimpressive genetic contributions. He cursed them for being poor and hated them for being content with squalor. The filth around him was not a cause for concern or even notice because it's what he grew up in. He knew no better way because he had not been shown.

The life path that Dustin was traveling down led to nowhere and yet he was only accelerating. Still too young to buy alcohol, he improvised with inhalants, cough syrups, over the counter meds and virtually any substance that would serve as an anesthetic. Recently, he'd begun scouring the sidewalks and parks for cigarette butts that still contained a small measure of smokeable tobacco.

After throwing on a hoodie, he left his apartment and

walked a few blocks toward the Maple Ridge Greenway. As he walked, he mentally scoffed at the people he'd seen sucking on Marlboros while wearing exercise clothing. The only physical effort he'd observed was their walk to the ashtray mounted on top of the green metal trash receptacles. His hands ruffled through the front pocket of his hoodie in hopes of finding a stray butt. A small blip of joy entered his mind as his fingers felt one lone straggler nestled in the dark recesses of his clothing. As he pulled the lighter from his pocket and joined it to the small paper cylinder, he let out an expletive. It was already down to the filter.

The Masons' Home,
Simmons Lane, Richfield

Mandy knocked on the door and delivered breakfast to her new tenant. A tray containing a small glass of orange juice, a plate of scrambled eggs, toast and fresh fruit, a fork and a decorative paper napkin was accepted by Helly, who recognized the generosity of her host. With her usual formality, she bowed and thanked Mandy.

"How much is the bill for you service?" Helly asked while holding the tray.

Mandy smiled quizzically. "Oh, for the breakfast! Sorry, I was confused. This is on the house. We'll talk later on today about your stay here and what that could look like."

Helly looked suspiciously at Mandy and then at the food. "What do you mean that this was on the house? Is food traditionally stored on the roof in America?"

Mandy finally caught the misunderstanding and accidentally let out a snort of laughter. "I'm sorry. There are a lot of things we say here in the States that must sound very funny to you. 'On the house' means that it's free. There's no charge."

There was contemplative silence as Helly digested this information, which prompted Mandy to expound. "I think it's a gambling expression. The casino is called The House and sometimes they offer free things to people who gamble. It sort of encourages them to stay longer and spend more money."

"Is that how you support your family? You operate a casino here in your home?"

"Nope. Being a housewife and mom is about all I can handle. No slot machines or roulette tables here - just a bunch of diapers and toys. Speaking of that, I've gotta get back inside. I usually pack Tom some snacks in his briefcase. He forgets to eat when he's really busy."

With that, Mandy turned and disappeared down the stairs. From the window, Helly could partially see inside of the kitchen through the back glass. Little Maddie was sitting in her high chair as Tom attempted to feed her. He appeared to be singing and was making faces as he bobbed the spoon around in circles toward her open mouth. Such a strange culture, Helly thought. And yet, it was beautiful to her.

Maple Ridge Greenway, Richfield

Helly had decided to revisit the only place she had some familiarity with, since Mandy was busy until noon. She retraced their previous route to the nearby park, where she immediately used the water fountain in the way that normal people do. She then surveyed the people using the public space. There were two older men playing a board game on a concrete table nearby. She assumed it was the strategy game known as chess based on the shaped pieces they played with. *I will learn and master that pursuit,* she concluded to herself. A large group of children were being led by two women, who were pointing out various types of wildlife. She could hear their questions.

"Now what type of animal is a squirrel?" Eager hands shot up in the air as faces displayed an urgency similar to one who desperately needs to relieve themselves in the bathroom. The lady pointed to one of the children and called her name. "Megan!"

The little girl looked very proud to be selected and said, "It's a mammal. It's warm blooded and does not hibernate in…"

The lady smiled and held up her hands. "Very good, Megan. Let's save some of the answers for the other students. Now, what type of food does a squirrel like to eat?" The hands shot up as the little ones again squirmed to be recognized.

As they continued on their way, Helly contemplated the severe contrast between Western schooling and her experience. Once again, she imagined what her childhood would have looked like had things been different.

She was presently wondering if the children were given any physical training when she saw two girls near her own age running at a sustained pace right beside one another. They were wearing athletic clothes and talking to each other. It did not appear taxing. She felt that she may be able to connect with these two ostensible warriors, so she stepped in front of their paths, forcing them to stumble to an awkward stop.

"Hello. My name is Helly. What discipline are you training in?"

The girls looked perturbed at being interrupted, both in terms of their momentum and conversation. Helly did not understand the value of smiling or how facial expressions can convey intention.

"Umm. I'm sorry but we are working out."

From her Western vocabulary training, she knew this term and tried to establish some mutuality. "Ahh. Pumping iron. Working up a sweat. No pain, no gain. I am familiar with these practices. May I join you?"

The girls looked at each other and shrugged. "Are you going to run in jeans?"

Helly looked down at her clothing and realized that her attire was not suitable for unhindered, sustained effort. She wanted to be accepted by them and realized that fashion, although shallow, did have significance. "You can give me a check for the rain. Maybe tomorrow. Goodbye." Helly was still obviously working on her colloquialisms.

-

Meanwhile, Dustin was making his rounds from trash can to trash can. He'd found at least a dozen smokable butts, 35 cents and a half a bag of Cheetos. He was popping one of the stale treats into his mouth when he saw her again. It's the girl from the fountain. Alone again and looking as lost as ever.

Dustin could have walked up to her and introduced himself. He could have expressed interest in her life, started a conversation and shown her respect as a fellow human being. Sadly, he'd had no example of that. The never-ending verbal and physical warfare between his parents had established a pattern of normalcy that would take a team of therapists years to unravel.

Deep inside of Dustin's mind were sentiments of spouses should provide something of value to you. Men were stronger and thus took priority. As provider and protector of the family, they deserve respect. Tragically, Dustin's dad was the provider and protector in name only. The only provisional deeds he had to his credit was the miniscule remainders of his monthly support check. Supposedly, not hospitalizing your wife was the equivalent of protecting her in his mind.

Unfortunately for him, he was unknowingly staring at Helly as she walked by. It's unfortunate because it caused him to ping on her threat radar. Quick glances and friendly smiles are universally accepted as normal, even to American girls who grew up in Chinese monasteries. Male drooling, on the other hand, was an immediate red flag. In accordance with her training, she continued on her way as if she didn't notice. However, her peripheral observations were noting his height, posture, distinguishing features, potential vulnerabilities and strike points. Not even an ounce of fear registered in her heart. The only processes in her mind were assessment and strategy.

John Cleveland

Main Street, Richfield, Close to Sunset

Mandy and Helly had enjoyed a terrific afternoon together. Virtual strangers, and yet their unspoken chemistry made them instant friends. As they shared stories from their past that had formed who they were today, Mandy pondered the fact that Helly was, by most standards, a foreigner. Yet, anyone who passed them would assume that they'd both grown up nearby. She watched as her young friend perused the storefront windows and all of the merchandise that was being proffered. She's grown up with only the clothes on her back and yet she turned out amazingly well. The thought left Mandy wondering if she should consider modifying her typical American way of parenting.

It suddenly dropped several degrees as the sun dipped down beneath the horizon. Mandy announced, "We should be heading home. I didn't realize we'd been out here so long." With that, she wheeled Maddie's stroller around and was trying to decide if they should retrace their route or take a shortcut through the industrial row. With trace amounts of ambient light left and cooling weather, she decided to shave some time off. A brief moment of silence fell upon them as they set off walking toward home.

As they passed by the first warehouse, the protective instincts in Mandy's mind began to spin. This area was not "as safe" as Main Street would have been. You're just being

116

an overprotective first-time mom, she thought to herself. That's when a shadow leapt from in between the metal buildings and landed not ten feet away, legs in a wide stance, arms held out with a glinting metal blade held in the right hand.

Already on edge, Mandy let out a shrill shriek and leaned over the stroller as she instinctively covered Maddie's body with her own. Her back was now fully exposed to the knife. She immediately began to plead. "Please don't hurt us! I have money! It's in my purse! Take it!" Her purse straps had become tangled in the stroller's handles as her shaky hands clumsily tried to hand it over. Her heart rate instantly doubled and her stomach was a churning pit of dread and fear. Her legs felt weak underneath her. Tears began to stream down her face as she began to sob over and over. "Please! Please. Please." Then Helly spoke.

"Do not give it to him. He is a coward. I can see it in his eyes." Her voice was flat and emotionless. Mandy's mouth dropped open as she looked up at the small form of her friend. Helly was expressionless and appeared to be analyzing their assailant with the same indifference she had used to examine the tool display back at the hardware store.

The dark figure's eyes darted nervously between the two young women. Better lighting would have revealed a sudden shaking in the blade. Helly stepped forward and to the left, now centered directly in front of the man who was at least twice her size.

"You can stay or you can leave. It makes no difference to me." Helly's words were eerily calm. Mandy couldn't decide if they were spoken to her or the attacker. The next few seconds trudged by in slow motion, an eternity when your heart is beating like a jackhammer. Suddenly and gratefully, the dark figure ducked to his left and disappeared once more into the shadows.

Helly turned to face the narrow alley and spoke to Mandy without looking at her. "Return to the Main Street. We will be taking the long way home."

Shell-shocked, Mandy mechanically pushed the stroller down the illuminated sidewalk. Her movements were blocky and automated as her eyes were focused only on the sidewalk directly ahead. Her breathing was erratic and shallow. She felt Helly catch up and match her pace in silence. Twenty feet later, Mandy stopped and looked directly into Helly's eyes. She searched for words that could only come close to being appropriate.

"You...saved us." And with that, Mandy began to sob again. Helly was not familiar with the customs expected after traumatic events, but Mandy completed the task for both of them. She wrapped her arms around the 17-year-old and hugged her tightly. Her body shook as she tried unsuccessfully to quell her crying. Helly felt Mandy's warm tears falling on her neck.

Helly stood there with her arms hanging loosely by her sides and immediately fell into the practice of mindfulness. What is this that I'm feeling? The sensation was completely new to her and not at all unpleasant. She felt a closeness that she'd never felt with another human. It was more than just physical proximity, although she felt like she was being smothered by a boa constrictor. It was a oneness. This friendship suddenly contained the added attributes of loyalty, devotion and exclusiveness. Mandy had experienced the threat of potential death and then miraculous salvation. Helly had spared a life and kept her clothes from being stained by another's blood.

It was another full minute before Mandy thought to call 911 and Tom. Shortly after, the area was bathed in blue and red flashing lights. The area was searched as the ladies waited in a marked police unit. Minutes later, Tom brought the Odyssey to a skidding halt that would have earned a traffic citation under other circumstances.

Later that night, when the excitement died down and everyone was trying to calm down enough to go to sleep, Mandy and Tom were having one of those solemn conversations that changes the course of the future.

"She is here for a reason," Mandy declared in the dark room as she stared at the ceiling. Tom was wise enough to remain silent, knowing that more thoughts would be spoken soon enough. "You know that 'all things work together.'" It was a quote from one of her favorite scriptures. "Oh God, what if we hadn't met at the park? What if I hadn't helped her at the fountain?" Her words now had two audiences.

Tom took the more rational approach. Although profoundly grateful that no harm had come to his family, he wondered if they would have been on warehouse row after dark if it had not been for their new houseguest. Humans have a strange and innate ability to find someone to blame.

With even more earnestness, she repeated, "She is supposed to be here. There's some reason we crossed paths. There's some reason I invited her to our home so quickly. You know I don't just jump into situations. You know I would never do anything that I thought might endanger Maddie."

Tom's mind considered myriad options and possibilities. He also pictured confronting an armed attacker barehanded. Surely, he also would have placed himself in between as a shield. Surely, he would have taken a blade to the gut to save his family. Right? However, one never truly knows until the rubber meets the road.

Silence lingered in the dark room as a mixture of troubled and grateful thoughts danced in the space above their heads. After a while, Tom spoke his approval of what Mandy had already decided. "She should stay."

Maple Ridge Greenway, Richfield

The next day, Helly arrived in style – matching light blue tank and shorts set with a high dollar pair of modern running shoes. With toned muscles and a slim waist, she very much looked the part.

While talking with Mandy the previous afternoon, she had explained her encounter with the two girls who seemed to be training and how they were dressed.

Mandy caught the picture and said, "I think I can help. Believe it or not, I used to be closer to your size before I started eating for two. But I wish Maddie had taken her leftovers when she was born!" She laughed loudly but was met with a blank look from Helly. Mandy realized this was wasted humor so she said, "I'll pull some clothes out for you tomorrow." Ever the optimist, she added, "Maybe you'll make some friends!"

The same two girls rounded the corner, jogging and talking with no perceptible sweat or discomfort. Again, Helly stepped directly in their path as they skidded to a halt.

"I'm dressed properly to run," she stated as leery eyes and snobbish faces examined her outfit.

"You almost got run over," one said with an obvious air of self-importance. She didn't want to be completely rude, so she continued with, "So, you're a runner?"

Helly was trying her best to learn American social customs and tried to use some street lingo she'd heard earlier. "Hey, crazy. I am usually capable of running as fast as my male counterparts."

The two friends exchanged quizzical looks with each other. The other seemed a little more compassionate and asked, "So what kind of runs do you do? 5Ks? Marathons? Halfs? Obstacle courses?"

Helly knew the pitfalls of lying, or even embellishing the truth, but she did want to make friends very badly. She chose the one that sounded the most like her training in the isolated mountains of China. "Obstacle course running. It is my favorite style."

The girls looked at the other with a grin that anyone else would have understood to be sinister. "Really? Obstacle course running. Ours too!" Their words were slow and exaggerated as if speaking to someone of lesser intellect. "Wanna do some training with us?"

Helly's lips involuntarily turned up into a smile. She was delighted to be included into this social circle and activity.

The girls nodded to each other, bladed their hands and then sprinted away at an impressive pace. Unbeknownst to Helly, both were big deals on their high school track and field team. They'd both placed in the state finals and were expecting scholarship offers from multiple universities.

Their form was impeccable – pushing off with the calve muscles, leaning forward, arms overexaggerating the movement to motivate their legs to keep up. It was an adage their coach used often: "Pump the arms, the legs will follow." It was impressive. Bystanders around the park looked at the out-of-place pair moving so quickly through the public area.

They had fallen into their stride. They well knew their limits and their lungs were nearing their redline. As the lactic acid began to build up in their leg muscles, they continued to push just to establish themselves as being in a higher league. They had covered just over 100 yards when one stole a look behind her, expecting to see the well-dressed "poser" growing smaller on the horizon as the distance grew. She actually tripped and almost fell to the ground, one shoe coming halfway off as she stepped on her own heel.

Helly was less than six feet behind them, mouth closed yet smiling. She was taking long, graceful strides that looked more flowy than determined. "I am enjoying this training. Will it incorporate any obstacles?" Everyone slowed to a stop as the pair tried to catch their breath and one refit her shoe.

Ego leaked from the two tracks stars like steam from busted boilers. Between gasping breaths, one said, "How...did you...do that?"

Helly gave a confused look resembling Spock from Star Trek when he did not understand common human behaviors. "Running is the normal progression from walking, which begins with crawling. I have been running, when allowed, since I was a small child."

The two girls were not mature enough to inquire about Helly's strange mannerisms or speech. Nor had they thrown in the towel. Their well-adapted lungs and legs were already recovered from what would have been a simple drill at practice. "You want obstacles? You got it." The same routine ensued. They looked at each other and nodded before turning to sprint away again. Helly grinned widely and followed after, looking like a graceful deer skimming across a field.

The two girls turned toward the woods with one taking the lead. As an empty park bench neared, the first lunged into the air with her left leg completely straightened out ahead, her upper half bowed like a clamshell and the right leg drawn up close to her hips. She sailed across the three-foot-tall obstacle, landed in full stride and then pounded heavily to slow herself down to a jog. Her friend repeated the movement effortlessly. Both looked backward hoping to catch a tremendous "fail" moment.

Helly negotiated the obstacle the only way she knew how. Still several steps away, she swept her arms upwards and then left the ground with both feet together, her legs extended like Superman. She soared headfirst over the bench with several feet to spare as her head began to tuck downward. She looked very much like a lawn dart preparing to bury itself in the dirt when, suddenly, she allowed her arms to make contact with the soil. Her body rolled like a wheel, becoming an incredibly small ball until her feet were underneath her again. With amazing momentum, she sprung up and floated almost magically above the ground. Still airborne, she adjusted her limbs so that as she touched down, her dash continued as if the bench had never been there.

The girls slowed further and then stopped with mouths agape. As they fought to control their ragged breathing, they said to themselves as much as to Helly, "Are you serious?!? What kind of freak are you?" Since their showy scheme had backfired, they were now defensive and hostile.

Helly, in her innocence, still did not realize what their intentions had been, so she answered in a way that she hoped would be cool. "I'm a super freak, super freak. I'm super freaky." No music. No melody. Just plain, spoken words.

Samantha's Home,
Simmons Lane, Richfield

Samantha was in the middle of a full-blown pity party. The boyfriend that she had dreamed about and so desperately wanted was becoming a huge source of drama. She had not fully admitted this to herself, because almost anything was better than being alone. For better or worse, Cody was the only thread keeping her from falling into the abyss known as Looserdom.

She sat on the window seat, hating her room. It was still decorated for a ten-year-old: dolls, colorful pictures, pom-poms. *Why do I still have those things? I didn't even make the squad.* With that, she picked one up and threw it angrily toward the trash can. She missed badly, only adding to her self-loathing. *I'm not a cheerleader, I'm not athletic, I dread being around my boyfriend and I'm too weak to do anything about it.* She pulled her knees up to her chest, wrapped her arms around her legs and buried her head. No one came to her rescue. The phone didn't ring with an encouraging call from a friend. Her mom didn't bring any cookies of consolation. She was just alone.

Out of the corner of her eye, she saw someone through the window. It was the girl from across the street. She lifted her head to get a better look at what her mind had already confirmed. *Now there is someone who might be as sad and lonely as me.*

Helly was blue indeed. She had been incredibly alone

125

in the monastery. The only girl amongst all the male trainees. All of her mentors had been men. Even though she agreed with their reasoning, they had sent her away. She had been holding it together for weeks and Mandy had been a Godsend (a word she would later learn). However, she was truly disappointed that her first opportunity to make friends with girls her own age had gone so badly.

Desperation and self-hatred can serve as powerful motivators. Samantha sprang from the window seat and ran down the stairs. The door flung open as she sprinted from the house, down the driveway and across the street. It was only the loose gravel that reminded her that she had forgotten to put on shoes.

Helly turned and examined the oncoming locomotive that was Samantha. The girl displayed a huge smile, which seemed incongruous with her red, tear stained eyes. Regardless, she did not register on Helly's internal threat radar.

"Hi! I'm Samantha," she panted. She stuck out her hand, which Helly shook with her usual stiffness. Fresh from her recent ridicule, Helly was especially leery. She remained silent. Samantha continued, "I saw you walking with Mandy the other day. I just love her." Samantha was still grinning and had crossed her arms as she wagged her head. "Anyway, what's your name?"

"My name is Helly."

"Helly? Like the clothing brand? I think I have one of their jackets. Love it!"

Helly had no idea what she was talking about.

Samantha was determined to make a friend. "So, are you visiting the Masons? Are you related?"

"We are not related. I met Mandy at the park and they have allowed me to stay in their apartment for the immediate future."

"I'm sorry. I know you're not supposed to ask things about people anymore." She rolled her eyes and made air quotes with her fingers as she said, "You might offend someone. But do you have an accent?"

"I am from China. My parents were American. They are dead and I do not know if I have any family here."

Samantha's smile faded into a look of genuine concern. "Oh my gosh. I'm so sorry." She put her hand against her heart, not because she wanted to appear compassionate but because she naturally was. After a moment, her brightness returned and she said, "Well, you've at least got a friend now, two including Mandy!"

Something happened in Helly's heart. Another new sensation. She quietly reflected on it and tried to discern what she was feeling. It was like Mandy's hug last night, but it felt more familiar, natural. This was a girl her own age. This girl could teach her how to be American. How to fit in. For a young girl who had done so well to survive, she found herself realizing and accepting this formerly unknown need. With no precedent for how to respond in a moment like this, she lunged toward Samantha and wrapped her arms around her in a bear hug. She could not mimic Mandy's tears or heaving breaths, but this would have to do.

Samantha, although momentarily shocked, wrapped her arms around her newest pal.

Maple Ridge Greenway, Richfield

The "speed twins" may not have wanted to be friends with her, but Helly still recognized the opportunity to train at the park. She felt particularly at home in the wooded areas as they reminded her of the Songshan Mountains, albeit with no jagged peaks, winter snow or predatory animals. After completing a series of movements and breathing exercises, she decided to explore the paths that wound through the trees and over the small creeks. She'd been thinking about the running style of the two girls before they put on their exhibition. It had been strangely monotonous and nonchalant. She tried to replicate what she'd seen by stiffening her arms at ninety-degree angles and moving her legs in more of a rapid marching movement. It felt awkward and rigid, but she didn't feel like drawing any more attention to herself today. Apparently, her graceful union with the terrain passing under the feet (and sometimes hands) was not as common here in the States.

Dustin had just settled into his nest. It was a small depression between three large oak trees. The underbrush was so thick around it that he had to crawl on his knees to access his "hidey-hole." A large piece of bark covered a small hole, which hid a light blue lunch box. It had belonged to a young boy who had left it on a picnic table while he explored a nearby playground. After swiping the box, Dustin justified his thievery with the thought that if the boy had truly wanted to keep it, he would have taken it down the slide.

Now it served as a vault for his stash. Inside was an empty flask that he'd found, some broken jewelry (probably fake) and a nudie magazine that had spent so much time out in the sun and rain that its models looked wrinkled and elderly. Nevertheless, it was forbidden fruit, which caused some inner part of his being to tingle. It was just the way he was wired. Given the choice between working for an hour or panhandling for three to pay for lunch, he would choose the latter. If stealing $10 worth of copper required $3,500 worth of vandalism, so be it. The perpetual victim, he felt no remorse for the losses of others.

Today, he was holding an open can of beer that still held a few ounces of liquid. He hadn't yet developed a taste for the fermented beverage but, once again, it was a forbidden fruit. After he nestled into his nest, he tried to find a comfortable position among the rocks, limbs and trees. He looked as if he was actually in a La-Z-Boy recliner watching a football game (sans furniture and TV). Once reclined, he slowly put the room temperature can against his lips and turned up the end. It was one of those baffling moments when what you suddenly taste is not what you were expecting. Immediately, he recognized a combination of stale beer, rainwater and old cigarette butts. He lurched forward and spat out the putrid blend, his shirt sleeve serving as an impromptu napkin. Next to exit his mouth was a series of expletives, which were heard by no one but himself. Still, the contents of his heart would spill out whenever he was jostled.

He slumped back against tree trunk and let his anger stew. *There is nothing good. Life is completely unfair and the people that have stuff don't deserve it*. He gave no consideration to the frugality or work of others. Anyone who had a car, nice clothes, a girl or anything he did not were viewed with a titanic load of resentment.

That's when he heard the footsteps. As always, when someone approached, he remained perfectly still and even quit breathing. No sense in revealing his secret lair. Through the branches, he saw her approaching. She rounded the curve in the paved path and was heading down toward the tunnel. *It's her! The fountain girl.* His mind had already fabricated several dark imaginations involving her. Sure, plenty of girls visited the park, but something about her was particularly appealing. Maybe her small size? Maybe her fit appearance? No, it was that she was alone. At that moment, his mind switched from fantasizing to planning. The steps of his strategy strung together naturally. All he really needed was a mask, a weapon and an absence of witnesses.

Samantha's Home,
Simmons Lane, Richfield

Samantha had turned on her most recent favorite song and was singing into a hairbrush with complete silliness. It had been playing on the radio at least once every thirty minutes due to its popularity. When the chorus came along, Samantha thrust the pink bristled "microphone" in front of Helly's mouth. Helly looked down questioningly at the beauty aid, her mouth closed and expression austere.

"Come on! You know the words!" Samantha returned the mic to herself and sang along as she bounced on the fuzzy rug. "I'm the moon, round and round, you're my world, we're so bound..."

Helly watched this Western custom and wondered about its purpose. As a matter of fact, the radio had been a mystery to her. From her brief exposure, it seemed to broadcast a mixture of music and assorted talking. The monologues were describing products that had the ability to drastically improve the quality of your life experience. The music had a lively beat but told stories with an elementary level intellect. She continued to study Samantha as she continued to sing into her brush. "I'm stuck in your orbit! Ooh, I'm stuck in your orbit, baby!"

As the song ended and a lady began to describe the debilitating effects that her old dishwashing detergent had on her hands, Helly asked her friend, "Are you preparing for a career as an astronaut?"

Samantha was catching her breath and looked puzzled. "What?"

"The song. It describes astronomical features. You seemed very excited about the prospect of exploring the heavens."

"Oh! The song. No. It's just the newest song by Sound Angel."

Helly's face remained deadpan.

"Sound Angel?!? Lexi, Toni and Tabi?!? Come on! You have got to be kidding me! They are going viral right now: YouTube, TikTok, Instagram."

"Are they in astronaut training?"

"No! Helly, I'm not trying to insult you, but have you been living under a rock? I thought they had American music in China. What about K-pop?"

"We had ceremonial drums, bells and horns. Mostly, there were chants that helped facilitate meditation. The rhythm assisted in slowing the heart rate and helping one find their inner peace. This music has an interesting and opposite effect. I find myself feeling energized and invigorated."

"Mission accomplished!" Samantha said as she shot a hand above her head like a rocket. She quietly reprised her space song as she opened her closet door. "So, in our country, um, your country, I mean, our country, girls usually share clothes. Check it out!"

Helly walked over and began to examine the assortment of shirts, jackets, pants and skirts hanging neatly on individual hangers. They were so colorful and vibrant. Until recently, her own wardrobe had been more monochromatic, consisting of an orange toga-like robe and sometimes a red sash. Her Western clothes still felt somehow restrictive and revealing at the same time.

Samantha pulled out a pink shirt with the word "Cutie" in large letters across the chest. She held it against Helly, frowned, and said, "Maybe we could ease into this one. Maybe something a little more subdued to get you started." She pulled out a white button up and layered it with a light jacket. "Now this sets off your eyes and hair. The white really frames you and the green jacket ties it all together."

Helly looked down at the jacket and saw the Helly Hansen embroidery near the left lapel. Her eyes widened with sincere surprise. "Do you know this person?" Helly urgently asked. There was a strange intensity to her voice.

"Who? Helly Hansen? I think it's just a clothing brand. Maybe it's the owner or designer or something."

Distant, cloudy memories emerged in Helly's mind as she rubbed her fingers over the stitching. It seemed vaguely familiar, even though she could not recall ever wearing such a garment.

They used the internet and read the history of the company on Wikipedia. Samantha turned to her friend. "You don't look very Norwegian to me."

The Masons' Home,
Simmons Lane, Richfield

As relationships deepen and mature, we use trust as a gauge of that closeness. Silently, we ask each other, sometimes on a regular basis, *Can you keep my secrets? Do you accept my flaws? Will you take my side? Will you still love me even if I let you down?* Or, you can just invite someone into your laundry room.

Helly wasn't put off by the piles of unwashed clothes, the bowl of pocket change and assorted knickknacks, or even the collection of lint that had accumulated in the corner. Instead, she marveled at the twin white cubes, which had the magical ability to not only remove stains and odors but to also restore garments to a wearable state. Mandy completed her demonstration by pulling a load of freshly dried towels out of the dryer and placing them into Helly's waiting arms. As the warm, billowy material engulfed her chest and face, she unwittingly buried her nose to inhale the subtle scent of flowers and rain. It was a brief moment of bliss.

Mandy observed Helly's reaction and wrinkled her eyebrows as she pondered how such a mundane task could elicit such a response. "Have you never washed clothes before?"

"Yes. It was a required chore at the monastery."

"So, did you guys not use fabric softener?"

"We did not use electricity."

Mandy's eye reflected her revelation. In her mind's eye,

she could see a young Helly carrying clothes to a creek's edge where she would scrub them with lye, slap them against the rocks and wring them out before laying them out for the sun to dry. Initially, she prayed a silent prayer of gratitude that she had never had to wash clothes in that manner. Then, considering the amazing, highly disciplined young lady that stood before her now, she confessed that it might have its own merit. Returning to the present moment, she said, "OK. It's your turn."

Mandy supervised as Helly separated the lights from the darks, inserted them into the washer and added a meticulously measured cup of detergent. As the knob was twisted and the start button was pressed, Helly turned toward Mandy as if waiting to be appraised. She stood there with a neutral expression as if she were prepared for praise, rebuke or further instruction. Realizing this, Mandy's reaction was a little over the top.

"Yay, Helly! Your first batch of laundry!" Mandy had made little fists and was now shaking them in the air. Helly looked perplexed. After an odd moment passed, Mandy spoke. "Sorry, Helly. I'm guessing that American accomplishments are probably a little underwhelming compared to what you've experienced.

"No. I am grateful for the instruction and the use of your cube."

Mandy cut her eyes toward the washer at this strange reference. "Well, it usually takes about forty-five minutes for a cycle. I'm going to fold some clothes upstairs and wipe down the bathroom. Would you mind keeping an eye on Maddie?"

Down the hallway, not twenty feet away, little Maddie

was entertaining herself in the living room with some toys that were scattered on the floor.

Helly faced Mandy, bowed slightly and answered. "Her safety will be my first priority."

The few minutes of peace away from a toddler were not going to be wasted. Mandy practically sprinted out of the laundry room and up the stairs, a basket of towels cupped in the right arm.

Dutifully, Helly turned her body so that she could observe the small child while remaining in close proximity to the laundry cube. She was determined not to fail in either of the newly assigned tasks.

Maddie quietly made noises and exclamations as she used her hands, mouth and eyes to explore her world. Helly could not help but to compare her upbringing with what she was seeing now. She remained alert and mindful but currently detected no threats in her vicinity...until she did.

Maddie had apparently lost interest in her toys and was crawling toward an object that Helly had been warned about since her youth. Her heart began to pound as the little legs and arms stretched to reach the forbidden object perched on the end table. "Maddie. No. That is very dangerous. That is strictly to be used by adults." The words might as well have been in Chinese. With absolutely no compunction, Maddie took hold of the television remote.

Helly's eyes grew wide. This was one of the first times since arriving in the States that she perceived the presence of mortal peril. She felt a deep obligation to remain with the laundry cube as it benevolently completed a task that she should be performing. However, Mandy had also charged her with the preservation and care of little Maddie. Making a decision, she decided that the clothes could be replaced more easily than a human child.

Quickly placing her hands on each side of the cube, she thanked the machine and prayerfully asked for its cooperation and understanding. To her horror, as she sprinted down the hallway, her worst fear materialized before her very eyes. Maddie had found the red power button and activated the television set.

In her civility and customs training, Helly had been told that children belonging to other people could not be touched, handled or reprimanded without expressed consent from their guardians. Her instinct was to slap the small black wand from Maddie's hand so that neither of them experienced the venomous infection that it so easily infused. However, the small child obviously did not realize the perilous state that she was now in. Plus, her cultural understandings forbade her to physically intervene.

Contemplating her options, she decided to shield Maddie's receptive eyes from the deceptive indoctrination. Positioning herself behind the child, she placed her hands just in front of her eyes. The little girl easily ducked away and repositioned herself. After several failed attempts, Helly moved between her and the television and held her arms up to block as much of the transmission as possible. Maddie giggled and simply moved to another viewing angle. Helly continued to twist and contort her body, which only made Maddie squeal with delight as she tried to replicate the strange movements. An elaborate dance ensued.

Flummoxed, Helly tried to swipe the remote, which had been dropped to the floor. Maddie quickly scooped up the device and was now determined to win this impromptu game of keep-away.

Curious about the joyful ruckus occurring without her, Mandy had crept downstairs and peeked around the corner. Her lips curled up into a smile as she covered her mouth to suppress a giggle. Maddie and Helly were engaged in a lightning-fast game of Twister except that there was no dotted mat and neither could touch the other. It was bizarre and beautiful to watch her little girl forming a bond with her new friend. Wanting to add to the moment, Mandy stomped into the living room and placed her hands on her hips before demanding, "What's going on in here?"

Maddie looked up, remote in hand and gleefully blew spit bubbles from a laughing mouth. Helly, however, snapped to a position of attention and bowed her head. Staring down at the carpet, an apology quickly spilled from her lips. "I have failed. In an attempt to keep your child from being exposed to evil, I abandoned my post at the laundry cube. I accept my responsibility and my punishment."

Never had Mandy felt the mood of a room shift so abruptly. Quickly deciphering the misunderstanding, she immediately shifted into repair mode. Dropping to her knees and taking Helly's hands, she looked up into the penitent face. "Oh, Helly. I am sorry. I was trying to be funny. I was upstairs cleaning when I heard all the laughter and I just wanted to be a part of it. I'm not upset."

Helly's eyes were processing this strange turn of events, but it obviously did not make sense to her.

"Please, tell me what you are apologizing for. I don't see anything that you have done wrong."

Helly gathered her thoughts before speaking. "I had intended to remain at my post with the laundry cube and assumed that I could watch the child from a distance. Then, your child saw the television device and was able to activate it. I could not remove the device because it is forbidden to physically correct another's child. In desperation, I was attempting to shield her eyes from the device's content." Her tone was remorseful as her eyes refused to rise.

Mandy took the remote and turned off the television. Maddie stumbled off in search of more mischief in the kitchen.

"Helly, please sit beside me." As she complied, Mandy continued. "I keep learning how different your childhood must have been. Heck, most kids here grow up glued to the television."

Helly frowned. "Is affixing your child to an appliance not frowned upon?"

"What? Oh. It's just an expression. They're not actually glued to the television. It's just that kids tend to really focus on whatever they're watching." Mandy looked distantly as she expounded. "It's like they're in a trance." Shaking her head, she returned her attention toward Helly. "It's probably not healthy, but I guess we get lazy. We let the TV babysit for us."

After processing this, Helly spoke. "As I was being instructed in Western culture, some of the strictest warnings related to the watching of television. We were told that it was a form of mind manipulation hidden beneath the guise of entertainment. We were told that it was the primary reason for American obesity, crime and apathy." She bowed her head. "I was trying to protect young Maddie."

Mandy's shoulders slumped. Suddenly, she felt like a horrible parent and an even worse friend. Turning to Helly, who would still not meet her gaze, she offered a very sincere, "Thank you. I can't tell you how much this makes me admire you and appreciate you."

Helly cautiously looked at her friend. "May I ask you a question?"

"Of course."

"Why did you appear so angry when you entered the room?"

Mandy thought for a moment. "I'm not sure. It's just something silly parents and even people do. You act like you're really mad and overreact to a situation. Then, when everyone else reacts to you, you quickly change course and begin to laugh and smile. It's supposed to be funny. We call it 'getting a rise' out of someone."

As always, Helly contemplated this with furrowed brows. "This method of comedy seems complex and risky. I will not attempt this until further exposure to your culture."

Mandy smiled as she felt the tension leaving the room. Helly seemed to accept these explanations, but contemplated them only for a moment. Suddenly, Helly's eyes went wide as her spine stiffened. "I must return to the cube at once!" Before Mandy could respond, a body flew like a whirlwind from the room and down the hallway.

Westwood Hills Mall, Richfield

The past three weeks had cultivated their friendship to the point where trust was expected, secrets were shared and Helly found herself smiling from time to time.

Samantha was animatedly moving her hands as she told a great story about last year's Homecoming Dance. "So, they hand her the microphone so that she can say what being crowned queen means to her and then Jason hits the remote for the fart machine. THHWWWWTTTTT!!!! She dropped the mic and ran off the stage!" Samantha was laughing so hard that tears came to her eyes as she struggled to complete the tale.

Helly thought about the situation and began to form a mental movie of the described events in her mind. She'd never been to a dance, but the television she'd watched recently helped fill in the gaps. As she thought, her head tilted and her eyes cut upward and to the right. A slight chuckle escaped from her mouth. She instinctively covered it as her eyes went wide. Samantha looked at her with a joyous shock. Then she laughed, which caused a positive feedback loop. Within seconds both girls were cackling, which led to the holding of stomachs and eyes squinched closed.

Both had found something they didn't realize they needed. Samantha yearned for a sliver of the inner strength she saw in Helly – never anxious, never intimidated, always in control of her emotions. Helly, on the other hand, needed exactly this. Silliness. Not only was it prohibited in the monastery but it was virtually non-existent. It had no place there. Now, wearing jeans and a t-shirt, she finally felt like she was blending in. Her mind was subconsciously learning and replicating the mannerisms she observed, repeating the idioms she heard and loosening up her posture...a little.

It felt good. Although she had no leads on any family, the friendships she'd forged with Samantha and Mandy were giving her a sense of completeness and security that all of the world's meditation and martial arts never could.

As they walked home that afternoon, Helly asked, "Why do you never speak of your betrothed?"

"My what?"

"I believe his name is Cody."

Samantha's eyes unconsciously dropped down and she began to look at her shoes as they plodded along the sidewalk. "Oh, you mean my boyfriend." Her tone of voice was as flat and emotionless as Helly's had been. "I think betrothed means something more serious, like in a biblical sense."

"So, you are not committed to this man?"

"We're committed, I guess. Like, we could change our minds and see other people...I think."

There was silence before Helly stated, "He appears to be a source of sadness for you. Was this relationship arranged by your parents?"

"What? No! They don't do that here. He's great, it's just that..." Samantha paused to formulate the right words. "It's just not what I was expecting." Helly waited for her to continue. "When you see people together in the movies and stuff, they're happy. They hold hands and laugh as they walk through the park. They gaze at each other over the table at an Italian restaurant. He tells her how his world was incomplete until he found her and then they kiss like the world's about to end."

Helly was absorbing this information.

"Me and Cody seem to only argue and it's like we're being forced to be together. It doesn't feel natural."

"But you are being honest when you say that your parents are not forcing you to marry this man?" She decided to add an American phrase she'd heard. "You can tell me. I can keep many secrets."

"No! I don't want to get married! Not now and not to him!" Her unprompted confession surprised even her.

"Then why have you obligated yourself to this man?"

Samantha continued monitoring her steps. After a moment, she responded. "I don't know. It's just what you do. I've seen my parents stay together when they don't really seem happy. Plus, I'm just scared that maybe there won't be anybody else. It's better than being alone, right?"

Helly's wisdom leaked out. "Solitude requires strength that few possess."

Samantha wasn't sure if it was encouragement, criticism or just more of her friend's strange sayings.

The two friends walked side by side in silence. There would be more talking later. Samantha put her arm around her friend's shoulder. It's seemed like it should be reciprocated, so Helly did the same.

The Mason's Home,
Simmons Lane, Richfield

That evening at the Mason's dining room table, three of them said "Amen" at the conclusion of Tom's prayer. Little Maddie did her best "Men!" which brought smiles from the others. The events of their days were shared and then Tom brought up a more serious subject.

"Helly, we have really enjoyed you being here. You've been such a big help to Mandy and I'd let you stay here forever after what you did that night for them...for us. But what do you see the future looking like? We won't have a teenage girl for over a decade, so this is a new situation for us. It's strange to think that we'll be having a conversation like this with Maddie in about fifteen years."

Helly had grown comfortable with the Masons and had no reason to mince words. It was not her way. Gratefully, this spared Tom and Mandy from some more difficult questions. "I have been giving serious consideration to this conjecture. I realize that I am not your daughter, have no claim to your assets and must progress toward independence."

Tom and Mandy exchanged bemused looks. Neither was expecting a response this mature or direct.

"One must contribute to the needs of their society in order to partake of its bounty. I have observed that America truly is the land of opportunity. In my research, most establishments are not available for inquiry of employment until after 9:00 AM. After I complete my morning training, I will attire myself and offer my services."

Tom had prepared to give a very fatherly talk about responsibility and growth, all of which now seemed obsolete. Instead, he awkwardly offered Mandy's help in preparing a resume and then chauffeuring her around town. Mandy stifled a slight glare at her husband for not checking with her first. Then, she reconsidered her ire because it actually sounded like fun. Besides, it would be good training for the future.

Maple Ridge Greenway, Richfield

The autumn weather was cooling off. Any other runner would have grabbed a light jacket and gloves today. Helly looked as comfortable and serene in her running top and shorts as if it had been a balmy summer day. She was deep in thought about what the day might hold as she applied for various jobs. Her current dilemma was trying to decide if she should act American or just be herself.

The chill in the air must have discouraged the other fitness fanatics because she had the Greenway to herself today. Just as well. She was very comfortable with solitude. As she rounded the curve, a familiar sensation began to glow in her stomach, up her spine and into her cortex. She was trying to recall the last time she'd felt like this. Then it came to her.

It had been at night, in the Songshan mountains. She had been tasked with fetching water alone. The ambush. The boys. In normal people, the brain would have signaled the production of the neurotransmitter glutamate. As it arrived in the hypothalamus, it would have released adrenaline into the bloodstream. Helly only felt a quickening, a heightened sense of awareness. Her ears became more attuned as her eyes began to absorb more data from the fringes of her peripheral vision.

–

His heart almost doubled its rhythm. There she is. His quarry had appeared. She rounded the curve, alone, her running shoes lightly pounding the pavement with the accuracy of a metronome. How sweet this would be. He couldn't wait to grab her from behind, put the knife to her throat and dare her to scream. Her eyes would go wide with terror and that smug confidence that she portrays would fracture into a mask of fear. She would fear him. She would respect him. She would submit to him.

He looked left and right to make sure the coast was clear before leaving his shadowy concealment. She was trotting down the grade and nearing the darkness of the tunnel. He picked up speed and closed the distance quickly. He tightened his grip on the knife and mentally practiced the move one more time.

The far end of the tunnel opened to a shady area where neglected trees and shrubs hung over the path. From there, it would be a short drag down to the stream's edge where sounds would be muffled and privacy was assured.

Fueled by adrenaline, he covered the remaining ten feet between them. To be this close to her in person, he was surprised by how small her frame was. He was at least 10" taller and probably twice her weight. All the better. Easy prey.

It went exactly according to plan. Right arm across her chest, left hand holding the knife against the neck, medium pressure, not enough to break the skin but enough to ensure immobility, silence and cooperation. He pulled her back to his chest and easily lifted her off the ground. In his adrenalized state, she felt unusually light. He moved to the right under the cover of pine branches and began to negotiate the gentle downgrade covered in pine straw. To his great relief, she didn't struggle or scream. So far, so good. His heart was pounding with excitement.

A faint signal of caution registered somewhere in his mind, but it was not immediately heeded. Only when she spoke did it garner his attention.

"Are you confident of your success?" It was her. She was eerily monotone, emotionless or maybe even bored. Her voice was so quiet as to be barely audible, but for some reason it filled him with the same punch of dread that a close lightning strike instills. His knees suddenly felt weak.

"Excess size can be a snare in warfare. You should reconsider." Again, that nonchalant attitude. Completely indifferent. *What is going on here? What is wrong with her? Maybe she has some type of emotional condition where she's unable to express fear?* Whatever it was, it was becoming very unnerving. He had expected her to panic, cry and even beg for her life. He had envisioned having total control of the situation, complete dominance. But now, he found himself questioning his position.

He made his way down toward the creek where he had located a flat, secluded spot. He had hoped to feel an immense sense of anticipation and excitement but did not. Instead, it felt like he was hopelessly trapped in a plan that was doomed to fail. His mind could no longer fathom a favorable outcome. A new surge of anger filled his veins as he thought of the unfairness of even this. Not even his highest moment of depravity could be enjoyed.

He still held her high so that her feet could not touch the ground as he turned around to make sure the coast was clear.

Suddenly, he was no longer holding the knife. His left hand would have throbbed horribly if it had not gone suddenly numb. *Impact.* His vision turned black as something struck between his eyes with incredible force. His stunned mind processed the scent of hair, which helped him to realize that she'd used the back of her head to break his nose. He reflexively doubled over as two small arms swung up past his ears and locked around his neck. Immediately, he felt his blood straining to pulse through restricted arteries. Then, he was flying, feet over his head as his chest fulcrumed over her small rounded shoulders. He landed hard on his back, gasping for breath between the shock to his body and exertion. As his eyes flickered open, he looked up to see her form springing from the ground and twisting in the air above him. Her right leg extended during the rotation and as she landed beside him on her rear end and hands, her heel came down hard on his sternum. Bones broke. Pain saturated his system like electrocution. If Dustin had been more acquainted with compassion, perhaps he would have mercifully passed out by now. However, he would have to endure a barrage of precisely targeted blows from elbows and fists, each causing injury that would later be noted on his hospital chart.

His consciousness finally surrendered, which was the signal to Helly that the threat had been neutralized. She scanned her surroundings for any other sources of danger before tossing what appeared to be a steak knife into the nearby stream. Satisfied that no other action was required, she retraced her steps up the hill and to the greenway where she calmly resumed her running. 911 would not be immediately contacted. She did not realize it was necessary to call the police, nor did she have a phone. It would be later that morning before curious walkers on the greenway would call, reporting moaning noises coming from the woods.

Main Street, Richfield

Thankfully, Mandy was sort of an aficionado when it came to creating a resume. As an English major with a bent toward administration, it came naturally to her. Since Helly had no formal work experience, they decided to capitalize on some of her imputed talents.

"Fluent in Chinese and English. Self-disciplined with a commitment to physical fitness. Attentive to detail with a temperate personality." Although there were no degrees or certificates (or diplomas for that matter), they printed her resume on some high-quality paper stock and used the trendiest formatting and fonts. At her age, a good first impression was more valuable than her resume's content.

They stopped by the fast-food restaurants, the bowling alley and the day care. Either they were fully staffed or she needed to be eighteen. Nevertheless, Mandy continued to gently coach Helly so that she could shake hands, make eye contact, introduce herself and even show somewhat of a smile. "Good manners will take you farther in life than skill or even intelligence," Mandy was saying.

Helly asked, "Is this a quote from an honored scholar?"

Mandy shrugged. "I don't know that my dad is an 'honored scholar,' but he did help me land my first job. I worked the continental breakfast bar at the Hampton on Saturday and Sunday mornings. Didn't pay much but I could keep any tips. I quickly learned that people skills pay off."

"When you say tip, you are not referring to the lethal end

of an arrow."

Mandy paused and made a mental note of yet another *Hellyism*. She and Tom had begun to keep a written list of the funny questions and quotes that came with teaching their houseguest the nuances of life in America. "A tip in the business world is also known as a gratuity. It's an additional amount of money that a customer voluntarily gives for excellent service."

Helly absorbed this, as she did all of Mandy's advice and instruction. Mandy continued.

"I don't think employees from other countries necessarily expect a tip, but here in the States, most service workers feel entitled to one. They almost strong-arm you at the register."

"Strong-arm?" Helly asked.

"Sorry. It's another expression. It means to force someone to do something without actually touching them."

This made little sense to her, but she accepted it along with everything else she was learning in this strange, alien world known as America.

"I need to stop by Buckston's to get a few things. Do you mind running in with me?"

"I would be glad to accompany you into Buckston's grocery store," Helly replied with her incredibly odd formality.

"That works, but you could also say something like 'Sure!' or 'Sound's great!' or 'Whatever.'" Mandy snickered at herself. "That's what a typical teenager would probably say."

As they entered, they turned left and waited in line at the customer service counter. Mandy had purchased a box of detergent that had somehow turned from powder into a solid block. Buckston's was always good about accepting returns and offering a replacement. It's one of the reasons she liked to shop there instead of the big-box stores. As they waited, they could easily overhear a conversation taking place between a young female employee and a man who appeared to be her manager.

"The guy gives me the creeps. And I barely understand him! He's always bossing me around, yelling in Russian and waving his knife around in the air. Did you guys even do a background check on him?" Her arms were crossed across her body, and the way her head was tilted to the side reflected the derisive tone in her voice.

"It's Chinese," the manager corrected. "English is his secondary language. And, yes, his background was checked before we hired him. The safety of our employees is our number one goal." The last line sounded a little bit rehearsed and insincere. Anyone who worked or shopped at Buckston's would also hear that "Saving the customers money," "Maintaining that neighborhood-market feel" and "Providing the city's freshest produce" were also their number one goals.

"And besides, nobody within one hundred miles can beat his sushi or seafood. Did you know that your department makes up for 12% of our total sales?" If this fact was supposed to stoke her morale, it failed.

With a roll of her eyes, she made her demands with the same aloofness as a Hollywood celebrity. "Transfer me to another department or I'm going to tell my dad that the conditions around here are unsafe."

The manager knew that her dad was serving on the city

council. He began to rub his forehead with his right hand while his left was perched on his waist. He silently cursed his managerial training, which did not include role play with sarcastic, spoiled dependents of city leaders. He caved.

"Look. There's no need to involve your father. Your safety is..."

She finished for him "Yeah, yeah, yeah. Your number one concern. Just put me in produce and move Billy to cleanup. He'd probably like mopping."

And just like that, a thirty-two-year-old man with a college degree took orders from a high-school senior.

As she turned and stormed away, Mandy and Helly heard him lament to himself. "Where am I going to find a replacement assistant for Chen? He can't prepare the fish and work the counter." He reached for a bottle of antacids and began to crunch down two of the orange tablets. Mandy and Helly exchanged glances that silently said, "Are you thinking what I'm thinking?"

In a move that surprised Mandy, Helly walked up to the manager, stuck out her hand and spoke.

"Wǒ huì shì yīgè héshì de tìdài zhě."

The recently ill and confused man gave a wary look to this young lady. She continued.

"It means 'I would be a suitable replacement.'" As she waited for a handshake, her left hand whipped out a resume seemingly from mid-air.

With mouth open and baffled eyes, he scanned the printed lines. He looked back and forth between the paper and the girl multiple times before he dumbly asked, "So, when can you start?"

Tater's Restaurant, Richfield

"To Buckston's newest employee!" Tom dramatically announced with a grand smile.

He raised his water glass into the air, which prompted Mandy to do the same. She nodded to Helly, who awkwardly repeated the motion with her glass. They clinked their cups together. "It's called a toast. And I don't mean the breakfast bread. Some people lightly bump their glasses together when they are celebrating something. You usually see it at weddings or awards ceremonies." Helly nodded in her customary way.

"Seriously, we are so proud of you, Helly. When Mandy told me about you overhearing their dilemma and being so assertive, I felt my chest swell up. It means that I'm very proud of you." Tom couldn't help assuming a fatherly demeanor with Helly. He frequently had to remind himself that she was not his. However, the place she had secured in his heart was almost paternal in nature. "You are making it obvious to us that you can handle yourself, but we want to support you any way we can. I've been thinking about a way for you to get back and forth to work without walking. We'll eventually work on some driving instruction but, in the meantime, I think I have a great solution." Tom sat back and relished his moment playing the wise father. That evening, the four of them enjoyed their celebratory dinner, because tomorrow - Helly would be joining the rat race.

The Mason's Home,
Simmons Lane, Richfield

It lay on its side in the short grass, taunting her and daring her to approach. She had faced multiple attackers, experts armed with nunchucks, swords and bo staffs. Even the darkness of night was no match for her dauntless courage. This, however, was proving to be her arch nemesis. An unconquerable enemy armed at every point with another menacing implement of injury. Metal horns protruded from its head end. A gleaming circular star of pointy death was affixed under its belly. Rotating blades at its front and rear threatened to remove an offered appendage as it rolled around on its rampage of death.

She stared at it, confounded and feeling closer to defeat than she had ever felt in her life.

"So, I guess you never learned how to ride a bicycle at the monastery?" Tom asked. He felt terrible seeing her frustration. He had offered his mountain bike as a way for her to commute back and forth to work without considering this one small detail.

With an expectation of mastering anything requiring balance and physical fitness, she had sat on the seat as the slightly sloped driveway began to pull her downhill. Like most newbies, she gave extreme inputs to the handlebars while completely forgetting to use the brakes. The bike began an exaggerated wobble that ended in a pile of legs, pedals and spokes. An immature frustration that she had not felt since childhood overwhelmed her bearing.

Since arriving in the States, she had seen numerous people effortlessly riding bikes, including very small children. While pedaling, they smiled and even conversed with one another as if it were as natural as walking. What Helly failed to grasp was that cycling required a unique blend of balance and light control. Instead of fighting it into submission, she needed to allow it some freedom as the centrifugal force of its spinning wheels would actually aid in keeping it upright.

Tom had developed the habit of seeing these moments as training for his own future. Helly would have to be the guinea pig as he floundered his way through fatherhood. As the moments ebbed by, he felt desperate to come up with a solution. Like most modern men, he whipped out his smart phone and searched for "How to teach someone to ride a bike." In a Matrix-esque way, he downloaded the technique into his mind and said, "I've got it." He made a quick trip to the toolbox and wrestled with the bike for a few minutes before announcing, "Alright, Helly. Follow me."

Helly approached the tubular terror as if it were a tiger defending its young. As she neared to observe the newly modified bike, she said, "You have removed the shin peelers."

"The what?" Tom asked.

Without a familiarity of bicycles, she explained. "The protrusions from the lower throwing star. The ones positioned to cause injury to one's shins."

"Oh," Tom smiled. "You mean the pedals. Yeah. Apparently, they just get in the way when you're learning.

Let's try something." And with that, Tom retrieved the bike, pushed it to the corner of their backyard and turned it around so that it was at the top of a small knoll.

"Alright, Helly. The article said to sit on the seat, hold onto the bars and let your feet lightly drag the ground on both sides as you roll downhill. That way, you can keep your balance and moderate your speed." Tom hopped on and demonstrated the method. He made a point of shouting "Whee!" in an effort to persuade her that this should be fun.

She was legitimately scared. The idea of her controlling such an unwieldly and dangerous contraption currently felt impossible. Had it not been for Tom's endearing smile and way he encouragingly nodded toward the bike, she would have abandoned this lesson. However, the male-female dynamic of their relationship reflected the psychological connection she had to her Shaolin laoshi.

Reluctantly, she straddled the dreadful beast and gripped its menacing horns. Her back registered the gentle push from Tom as the bike began to gain speed. Her heart rate almost doubled and her eyes focused on the handlebars, the grass picking up speed as it passed underneath. She dragged her feet, which caused the bike to totter, but then she evened out the pressure. She found that gentle inputs on the horns, um...the handlebars, could correct the direction, thus making it possible to control. As the slope leveled out, the bike rolled to a stop.

No crash. Helly was elated. A broad smile spread across her face as she involuntarily turned to see if Tom approved. He was running downhill, his big smile matching hers in size. He stopped right beside her and held his palm up in a vertical position.

"Way to go, Helly! Tom exclaimed. "You killed it!"

Helly, still smiling, was suddenly puzzled. *What have I killed? Should I replicate this gesture?* So, she released her right hand from the bar and held it vertically in the air. Suddenly, Tom rushed his hand towards her, resulting in an audible *SLAP!!!* Tom appeared to be pleased, so she made a mental note of this ceremonial movement.

A few more runs down the hill and then Tom reinstalled the "shin peelers," as he'd begun to call them.

"Alright, Helly. This time, once you feel comfortable, put your feet on the pedals. It will be just like before, but one step closer to taming this beast."

It reminded her of the first time she'd handled a real sword instead of the wooden training stick. There were real consequences for failure. But Helly felt different now. With her little bit of experience and Tom's supportive presence, she knew she would succeed.

The bike began to roll forward and she lightly dragged her feet on the ground as before. She felt the bike becoming more stable with speed, so she lifted her legs and positioned her feet on the pedals. It wobbled only once before yielding to its new master. Without further instruction, she spun her legs, which easily overcame the tension of the chain. The mechanical propulsion spun the rear wheel and sustained her momentum. She pedaled smoothly and could hear Tom shouting behind her as her pace began to outdistance his.

"WOO HOO!!! GO HELLY!!!" Tom bellowed.

She crossed the driveway and rolled across the front yard. To her right, she could see Mandy standing on the front porch holding Maddie on her right hip. She held Maddie's hand and waved it triumphantly while speaking for the little girl, "Great job, Helly! You got it!"

It was one of the best moments of her life, possibly number one. In her heart were two competing emotions, one which savored the feel of Tom, Mandy and even Maddie's pantomimed applause. It was so sincere and seemed like the transfer of light from one soul to another. The other was a sadness at the realization that she could have had this whole time if her childhood had been different.

The moment of daydreaming was just enough of a distraction for Helly not to notice the approaching mailbox. With no instruction on how to brake, the front tire struck the wooden post with the force of a sledgehammer. However, Helly was no longer under the oppression of fear. She could now influence the outcome of this collision. Tom, Mandy and even Maddie let their mouths drop open as they watched her spring up from the bicycle like a pilot ejecting from a fighter jet. Helly shot her arms straight as her body began a graceful arch over the asphalt of the street. Simultaneously, she tucked her head and positioned the back of her wrist so that they made contact with the pavement first. With the smoothness of a panther, she rolled and popped up onto her feet, the momentum carrying her upward off the ground.

All eyes turned to see a fast-approaching car, which was now braking and swerving, its blaring horn harmonizing with its screeching tires. Helly lengthened her body and appeared to be defying gravity partially by her will. Instead of bouncing off of the windshield as everyone expected, she sailed over the top of the car while contorting her body to avoid any contact. As the car teetered past with a *WHOOSH*, Helly landed backward on her feet. Effortlessly, she completed a back hand spring to exhaust her inertia and then landed in a crouch across the street in the neighbor's yard.

Tom and Mandy's faces were locked in expressions of terror. He had been sprinting toward her as the near disaster unfolded. He cleared the span of the road in three bounds and was preparing to console what would undoubtedly be a terrified teenage girl. Instead, he stopped quickly and found himself staring into eyes that were confident and calculating. He suddenly felt like a defenseless sheep that had stumbled upon a hungry lion.

Helly stood up slowly and allowed her hands to lower from in front of her sternum to her sides. Even though she was nine inches shorter, Tom sensed that he was in the presence of a power greater than he possessed.

"Are you OK?" he stammered. Helly took a moment to assess her surroundings: the departing car, the spinning wheels of the fallen bike, the slightly canted mailbox.

"Yes. I am now able to ride the bicycle."

Pinheel Drive, Richfield

At Tom's request, Helly was now wearing a pink, floral print plastic helmet. It was Mandy's and had been coated with a thin layer of dust from lack of use. Riding around the neighborhood, she silently scolded herself for previously being intimidated. She reasoned that it would have been an easier skill to learn when she was smaller and her center of balance was lower. No matter. Now, it obeyed her every command and provided her with transportation that was many times faster than walking. *American ingenuity at its best,* she thought. Little did she know that it was actually a German inventor, Karl von Drais, who had developed the Swiftwalker or Dandyhorse, as it was called.

She explored the neighborhood and experimented with leaning as she navigated each corner. Things were going well until another cyclist rounded the curve ahead, approaching in the oncoming lane. Had Tom been a better instructor, he would have explained that the bike will instinctively go toward whatever the rider is looking at. He would have warned her not to fixate on obstacles but to avert her eyes in a safer direction. This lesson would be learned the hard way.

As the other rider approached, she was instantly fascinated with his bike and clothing. The bike had a small front tire and a normal size rear tire. The seat was elongated, like a banana, and was positioned at the far back of the bike. The handlebars stuck up unusually high in the air, which made its rider look like a chimpanzee hanging from a tree limb. The metal of the tubing was gold in color with shiny ornaments and reflectors attached along its length.

She assumed it was a boy by his basic facial structure, but much of it was obscured by a huge pair of mirrored sunglasses. The cheeks were partially covered by a large fur collar that was silver in color. The coat that it was attached to had a bold purple paisley pattern that would have been right at home in a children's fantasy book. The jeans had additional pleats and folds that looked like multiple pairs had been interwoven together.

In her captivation, she failed to realize that she had veered toward him and was now on a collision course.

"Hey! Look out!" yelled the other rider as he swerved right and stopped against the curb.

It was a near miss. Helly quickly stopped and looked back to see if she had injured him.

With a practiced coolness, he looked over his shoulder as he lowered his shades to reveal eyes that were very familiar to her. He was Asian. His skin had a pale yet slightly olive tone that set off his dark, almost black eyes. If Helly had been more familiar with teenage boys and testosterone, she could have seen that the presence of a beautiful girl had bolstered his bravado. Instead of anger or shock, he had quickly assumed an air of machismo and intrigue.

"Hey, gorgeous. There're easier ways to say hello."

Helly furrowed her brows as she tried to interpret this pickup line. With her formality and staccato English, she said, "I am very sorry. I have only recently learned how to operate the bicycle." Looking very American as she did but sounding foreign, it was easy to assume that she was mocking his ethnicity.

He suddenly looked hurt and offended. "Very funny. Almost kill the Asian guy and then make fun of him. Unbelievable." With that, he pushed his glasses back into place and shook his head in disgust. He was about to ride away when she spoke again.

"My name is Helly. I was raised in China. I am new to the United States."

He redirected his gaze toward her, looked her up and down and appeared to be examining this statement for sincerity. He then kicked down the kickstand, dismounted the bike and sauntered up to her. He walked slowly with one foot almost crossing over the other with each step. His arms hung loosely as he walked, not really synchronizing with his gate.

As he neared, he once again made a big show of slowly removing his glasses. After an intentional pause, he made a quick nod with his head as he asked, "Are you for real, girl? Cause if you're casting shade on my people, then I might have to throw down. Maybe not with my fists because I don't do that domestic violence thing, but on my channel. You don't want that kind of publicity."

None of this made any sense to Helly, not his words and definitely not his mannerisms. It's like he was moving in slow motion, as if wading through water.

"If you have a channel, my friend may recognize you from her television set. Are you a news reporter?"

His eyes reflected his confusion and suspicion. Helly looked completely Caucasian. Yet, nothing else about her was: not her speech, not her demeanor and definitely not her jargon.

"Wǒ jiǎshè nǐ huì shuō zhōngwén," she said.

After a pause, she translated. "It means, 'I assume that you speak Chinese.' However, I now assume that you do not."

His face took on a look of astonishment. He actually leaned closer as if examining a visiting alien. "Whoa. You're the real deal, yo. Where are my manners?" With a flourish of his hand, he bowed slightly and said, "You now have the pleasure of meeting Bruce Levin, a.k.a. Hebruce Lee, as I am known on YouTube." He smiled slyly as he awaited any recognition. Her blank stare was immediately deflating. "Hebruce Lee? The voice of the Richfield Youth? The defender of minority religious disciples?" The silence of obscurity hung between them. "I'm an influencer. Just passed one hundred thousand followers."

Helly stared back blankly. "My friend has mentioned this YouTube and speaks of it as a distributor of information and entertainment. Is this the business you speak of?"

"Well, I just got monetized this year so, yeah, it's my business."

"How is it that you are monetized? I am familiar with the term but not in the context of your tube."

He blinked away what could have been a very vulgar and childish innuendo. "If you get enough likes and subscribers, companies will advertise on your channel. You get more money when more people like you. You really are for real. You didn't grow up in the States."

"I was raised by monks in a monastery in the Songshan Mountains. I was sent here to locate and re-establish any family relations I may have."

He blinked in an exaggerated manner while pulling his

head backward. It gave the effect that he'd been hit with a small shockwave. "Wow, girl. I cannot even imagine. You're like the perfect fish out of water story. Man, they wouldn't believe you on my channel." Suddenly, he smiled at the thought. "You know, I could make you famous. We could call you," he thought for a moment, "the American Imposter or…The Chinese Champion. I don't know. Nicknames sort of have to come to you. You can't force 'em."

"You said your name was Bruce Levin and then you said it was Hebruce Lee. How is it that you have two names?"

"It's like I said, girl. Bruce is my legal name but Hebruce Lee is my handle, yo. It's my channel name."

"What does it signify?"

"Well, I was born in China but I don't remember any of it. An American family flew over and adopted me right after I was born. It's turns out they were Jewish so I guess I am too. Put it all together and you get HEEEE-BRUUUUUCE-LEEEEE!!!" He said it with a deep voice that was meant to sound like it was echoing through a stadium.

"It is a pleasure to meet you, HEEEE-BRUUUUUCE-LEEEEE!!!" Even with her loud mimicking, her face was completely neutral.

He was at a loss. The awkwardness of their communication made him feel a little silly and immature. "Tell you what, Helly-Knievel. Here's my card. Maybe you could throw me some digits." As soon as he said it, he realized that she would not understand. "Maybe you could call me, you know, on the telephone. Maybe I could help you look for your family." It was his first step toward civility since they'd met.

"Thank you. I would be deeply grateful for your

assistance."

Buckston's Grocery, Richfield

The meat cleaver came down with a definitive clunk, the fish head instantly separating from its silvery body. With the quickness of a magician, the large knife was replaced with a smaller filleting blade. It spun like the baton of a majorette in the nimble fingers before slicing down the length of the belly and then back up through the entrails. The inedible portions fell out and were swiftly shuttled away before the blade made two more passes, separating the meat from the skin.

Helly watched with studious attention but not astonishment. It would not be a difficult task to repeat. However, her accuracy in replicating the technique would demonstrate her gratitude for the instruction.

With the two expertly carved flanks displayed on the cutting board, the stocky butcher relented his position and indicated with a grunt that she was supposed to attempt the procedure. He lifted his chin and actually groomed his goatee with a downward stroke of his right hand. He then crossed his arms and glared down at his *next-to-quit-and-run-away-leaving-a-trail-of-tears* trainee.

Helly took his place and let her hand float over the assortment of blades arrayed on the counter. Then, with the smoothness of a surgeon, she hefted the cleaver and rolled it with her wrist as if measuring its balance. Before the human eye could register, the head of the next fish disappeared from its body and rung the nearby slop chute. Again, seemingly like magic, the large chopping blade was instantaneously replaced with a smaller one. The carving knife moved with the quickness and accuracy of a laser guided CNC machine, its tip flipping the freshly cut pieces, which fell like parallel parked cars on the cutting board. Helly somehow spun the knife around the backside of her hand, reversed her grip and then sunk the blade deep into the wood so that it vibrated tightly from side to side.

The eyes of her instructor widened involuntarily, whereas Helly's remained unmoved and emotionless. Thus began her successful apprenticeship under the guidance of Chun, master of Buckston's seafood department.

The Feeding Trough, Richfield

This place would definitely score a 1, Samantha thought as she looked around the farm-inspired restaurant. She was imagining how her fellow diners would rank its "romantic setting" on a Google review. She looked across at Cody, who was sloppily finishing off his third plate of barbeque smoked wings, the sauce leaving a deep red ring around his mouth. They had only been dating for two months, but it had already become ritualistic and predictable. She felt elderly with him. She allowed the light from the images converted by her retinas to search her heart for any fondness of this man. *He bought me wings. That's something. He didn't ask for gas money but I'm pretty sure his mom pays for that. He's never hit me.* As far as desired qualities in a potential spouse, she had to admit to herself that she was aiming pretty low.

"Helly and I hung out this week," she said to break the silence. Cody jerked his head up from the plate, looking stupid and clownish.

"Helly? Who's that?"

She had mentioned Helly before in conversation but, obviously, it wasn't important enough for him to remember.

"The girl from China I was telling you about. She's staying with the Masons across the street." No recollection. Just blank, dumb eyes. *Why am I with him?*

"Is she hot?" he asked as his attention returned to his plate.

"I think she's really pretty." *I should not be in this relationship.*

"Is she, like, exotic or just kinda...foreign?"

Isn't this a strange thing to ask the girl you're dating? "She's nice...and interesting. How she looks is unimportant to me."

"Must be an uggo. You always say a girl is nice when she's ugly."

I feel so trapped.

The Mason's Home,
Simmons Lane, Richfield

"I hope she brings home more salmon!" Tom exclaimed as he rubbed his tummy, a big grin on his face. He'd been washing brightly colored children's bowls and overly rounded spoons in the sink.

Mandy nodded as she replied, "That has been a really nice perk. She's probably brought home $50 of fish since she started. I always thought it would be nice to work somewhere where you get the food they're going to just throw away."

"So, do you still feel like this is working?"

Husbands and wives develop a mental connection so that each other knows the topic of discussion without needing a reference.

"I think so. Yes. I don't think she's interrupting our lives." Mandy listed the benefits out loud. "She's extremely helpful to me around the house and with Maddie. Then, there's the whole *personal bodyguard* thing. Plus, the salmon." She was joking, but both of their stomachs were rumbling, so only half joking.

"Me too. I was not expecting this, well, *her* to be a part of our lives right now, but it feels like wonderful practice for the future. When she finally figured out the bike, I felt so incredibly proud, just like when Maddie took her first steps." His expression became reflective and distant. "And then there was the car thing."

Mandy put her hands on the counter and bulged her eyes. "I know! Was that not the craziest thing you've ever seen? Anybody else would have been flattened like a pancake, or at least traumatized. But to her it was like, 'No big deal.' She is unique to say the least."

As Tom turned toward the sink to rinse the last bowl, he offered solemnly, "She's special."

Buckston's Grocery, Richfield

Helly could not have been a better fit for the seafood department. She and Chun worked together like Siamese twins. They processed orders with silent, military precision. If a slab of fish was thrown blindly, Helly was instantly there to catch it. Every movement was fluid as if they were performing some well-rehearsed choreography. It kind of became a "thing" in Richfield. The first customer to witness the spectacle was sweet Mrs. Petty. As knives flashed and heads rolled, she felt as if she was watching a Hibachi show like you'd see at a Japanese steak house. Since Mrs. Petty was a socialite (a polite way of saying she gossips), word spread quickly about the duo.

The manager of Buckston's was elated. Sales were up 26% this week in the seafood department. It had been their quarterback but was now officially their MVP. He was already thinking about how to advertise their newest addition, or at least capitalize on her entertainment value.

Helly enjoyed the precision. She loved how nimble and familiar the knives felt. She thought back to her first lessons in weaponry. She was ten years old, sitting cross legged on the floor of the monastery. Her instructor continued:

> "The blade is silent. It can be reused immediately with no reset. Its length can be useful and adaptable, either long or short. A

single piece of steel is vastly more dependable than a machine of many parts. It signifies proficiency in combat. The Western armies allocate roughly two weeks for basic marksmanship. They are trained in massive herds with the weaker warriors intermingled with the stronger." He paused as he walked between the rows of young trainees, only one being a female. His voice took on an edge. "You will live with the blade. It will never depart from you. It will become an extension of you. Ironically, as your skill with it increases, the likelihood that you will need to use it decreases."

Her thoughts returned to the present as she caught a thrown mackerel. With a fair amount of fanfare, it was expertly wrapped in paper faster than it could be tossed into a bag. As the small crowd watched in awe, Chun nodded his approval. Helly felt completely at home.

Samantha's Home,
Simmons Lane, Richfield

Helly knocked on Samantha's door. They were supposed to hang out this evening. Her friend opened the door and rolled her eyes.

"Cody is here. He insisted that I introduce you."

Helly was perplexed at her friend's melancholy demeanor. As they neared Samantha's room, they heard the floor squeaking and someone grunting in a rhythm. As they opened the door, Cody appeared to be standing up from the floor. His reddened face showed exertion as he dusted his hands off. As he saw Helly, his chest seemed to swell up like a mating bullfrog.

"Were you doing push-ups?" Samantha innocently asked.

"No! I mean, nah. I thought I saw some, uh, a cat under the bed."

Helly walked up to him with her robotic mannerism. "Hello. My name is Helly." She stuck her hand out formally.

Cody was determined to be smooth. He took her hand and flipped it palm down before bowing down slightly. "Enchanté," he said, with a strange attempt at an Asian accent.

Helly frowned at the oddity of it. Samantha wanted to jump out of the window.

"So, Samantha tells me that you're into fitness. Me too.

I work out and stuff, mostly lifting." He made a fist with his right hand and gave a half-flex as if he were offering credentials.

"I have learned how to ride a bicycle but it is more of a matter of efficiency than an exercise in endurance."

Cody nodded dumbly, unable to form a suitable response. "Yeah. That's cool."

There was an awkward pause as Helly just stood there, confident and solid. Samantha stood off to the side like Cinderella in house-cleaning mode. Cody regrouped and launched another charm assault.

"So, I'd like to show you around Richfield, you know, give you a tour. Have you heard of The Feeding Trough?"

Samantha's hand went to her mouth in shock after hearing her boyfriend ask out her best friend right in front of her.

Helly asked, "Are you not betrothed to Samantha? Is it customary to court two young ladies simultaneously?"

Cody had overplayed his hand but was too dumb to realize it. "Well, me and Samantha are more like friends and I would just be taking you out to be nice."

Samantha made a sound like she was holding back vomit. Helly turned toward her friend. "I am not familiar with the customs of young men and women in this country. Should I accept his invitation? Is this socially acceptable?"

Samantha's mouth finally caught up to her mind. "NO! IT IS NOT ACCEPTABLE." Her usually bright and joyful countenance cracked into a mask of indignation. She locked in on Cody. "You need to leave. You need to leave me alone. You need to leave all women alone! You are..." She searched for an appropriate word, "A PIG!"

Cody's veins were still coursing with ego and machismo. In his infantile mind, there was still a chance that Helly would be into him. He stood there stupidly hoping for some spark to appear in her eye. The only gaze that returned was cold and emotionless.

"Do you want me to escort him out?" Helly asked her friend as if offering a refill of cola. Cody looked confused and then amused. He sneered and snorted.

"But, you're a girl. And a small one. Nobody will be escorting me out. I'll leave when I'm good and ready."

Samantha was fuming and marched straight toward him. In a moment of senselessness, he grabbed her by the shoulders and shoved her onto her bed. His eyes registered a flash of movement just before his lights went out.

Samantha and Helly leaned over and looked down upon the unconscious form of Cody lying on the floor.

"Is he dead?" Samantha's shaking voice asked.

"He is not. Would it be best to eliminate him?"

"No! We can't kill him! You can't just kill people in the United States. You'd go to prison. WE'D go to prison."

Helly nodded her understanding.

"And what was that?!? You spun in the air...like a helicopter! Did you mean to kick him in the head?"

"It was an available target."

Cody groaned as his head began to loll. His eyes flickered open as he began to recall the introduction, the weird rejection, pushing Samantha and then his world going dark. "What...happened?"

Samantha lied. "You tripped and hit your head." She

shot Helly a look that said *Trust me. Go with this.*

"I'm sorry, baby. I think it's this new pre-workout I've been taking. It makes me, like, crazy aggressive." He actually flexed his chest and made a smoochy face.

Samantha simply pointed to the door. Cody slowly stood and was shakily making his way to the door when he turned to cast one more hopeful glace at Helly. As he did, she simply pointed to her head in the exact spot where her kick hand landed on his. Somehow, despite his brain fog, he understood this to be a warning.

Hebruce Lee's Home,
520 Pinheel Drive, Richfield

The next day, the girls rode their bikes to the influencer's house. Samantha had not understood what Helly meant as she described her run-in with Hebruce Lee. It sounded like another one of her language misunderstandings, especially with the description of his fashion and style. However, when he answered the door, all the pieces suddenly fit.

"Wuz up, girly girls?" He let his shoulder slump against the door frame as he slowly lowered his shades.

"Hello, Hebruce. This is my friend, Samantha. She is familiar with the YouTube."

He nodded slowly and let out a long "Riiiigggghhht."

"Are you still able to help me find my family?"

Well, I can't. But my people probably can. Follow me." With that, he pushed his shades up and turned to go into the foyer. They followed him up the stairs through a very traditional home. However, when they pushed open his bedroom door, they entered another world.

The walls were covered in shiny, silver tinsel. There was a huge cutout of his head in black and white positioned on the wall over a desk of sorts. On its sleek black surface was a professional style microphone that was attached by springs to its pedestal. Nearby were two open laptops with programs showing an audio mixer program and some broadcasting software. Also on the desk was a golden trophy which read, "Hebruce Lee, 100,000 subscribers, March 25, 2025." The whole room was cast in blue lights, which shined down from various corners of the ceiling. An aquarium, also backlit in blue, was softly bubbling on a nearby stand.

Hebruce sat down in a modern high-backed office chair and put on a set of large, black headphones. He explained what he was doing as he typed. "So, 100,000 people know millions of people. But first, we need to make them care about who you are. All those suckers who ask for money on Kickstarter with no backstory are just wasting their time. You gotta get their hearts, yo, before you get their help."

He brought up a new screen and entered a few commands. Then, he grabbed a small, boxlike camera on a small tripod and set it up facing two empty chairs. "You feel like some footage?"

Samantha asked, "You mean, like an interview?"

Hebruce blew out so that his lips made a flapping sound. "That's for suckers. Live, one-take videos are forgotten as quickly as they are watched. We're talking a full-blown exposé, fully edited, Hebruce Lee style. We'll cleverly introduce her, you know. Get the audience's attention. Then we'll set the hook with some heartwarming details. Then, we reel 'em in with how she's looking for her lost family. Then we clean 'em and fry 'em with a few thousand "likes" and "subscribes."

Helly was lost on the urban lingo and social media terms, but Samantha's dubious expression spoke for both of them. "Are you trying to help her or just get more fans?"

Hebruce winced and pantomimed a painful effort to remove a knife from his heart. "Ouch! I'm trying to help the girl. If I wasn't popular, I couldn't help anybody. Cut me some slack." It was amazing how easily he could play both the capitalist and the victim.

Samantha shrugged her shoulders as she looked at Helly as if to say, "He makes a good point."

Hebruce pressed a few buttons and adjusted the microphone so that it would pick up both of their voices. A red light came on the camera. Helly sat there pleasant but impassive. Hebruce began.

"Look into the camera and introduce yourself."

"Hello. My name is Helly."

"Do you have a last name?"

"Hansen."

He'd been watching the screen of the camera but leaned around to look at her. "Are you serious? Helly Hansen? Like the clothing brand?"

"I have seen the clothing you speak of. Perhaps it is a coincidence."

He returned to his monitoring. "So, tell us where you grew up. Tell us about your childhood."

Helly paused as if arranging her memories and prioritizing them in terms of relevance. "I was probably born in America to American parents but I came to be in a monastery in China. That is where I grew up."

"Do you know how you ended up in China?"

"As a small child, I was told by my teachers that I fell from the heavens. However, when I reached a proper age, they expounded on the details of my discovery. It seems that my family was traveling in a small, private aircraft which crashed while attempting to traverse the Songshan Mountains. I had been placed into a suitcase that helped me to survive the collision. Because of the political environment at the time, my teachers chose not to surrender me to the local government but to raise me as they would a trainee."

"What type of trainee?"

"A monk. Specifically, a Shaolin monk."

"You mean, like, the martial arts experts? The undefeatable warriors?" He let out an incredulous snort. "Yeah right."

Helly was oblivious to his sarcasm and continued. "It was their hope that I could be reunited with some family relations in America one day, so in addition to my normal instruction, I was indoctrinated in Western Culture as they understood it."

Hebruce nodded to himself with the realization that this story was turning into pure gold. A small part of him suspected that this was all a hoax that his immature friends had cleverly arranged, but the greater part of him believed her.

"We received traditional instruction including grammar, history, science, combat, art, music, literature..."

Hebruce shook his head as he interrupted. "Hold it, hold it, hold it. Did you say 'combat?'"

"The Shaolin have been forced to defend themselves for centuries. Their isolation serves as a protective hedge which also demands total self-reliance."

"So, are you saying you can flip in the air and fight with swords and all that stuff?"

"It would be rare that a confrontation would require both activities simultaneously."

The lack of denial or confirmation only heightened his curiosity. Sadly, his bravado took over at this point and commandeered the conversation.

"You know, I'm working on my San-Kyu."

Helly stared blankly, which caused him to expound.

"You know, my brown belt? Third rank?"

Helly remained bemused.

"Karate? Martial arts? Like you." He looked hurt and deflated.

She asked, or maybe just confirmed, "You are a student of martial arts."

"Yeah, like you. We should spar down at the dojo sometime. I could show you some things." He wore a smug grin, which dissolved instantly as she flatly answered.

"But I am not a student."

Buckston's Grocery, Richfield

A traveling salesman had been working in Richfield for the last two weeks. Life on the road had become his lifestyle, so adapting to new towns and environments came easily for him. Whenever he was back at their home office, he deduced from seeing his rotund co-workers that sitting on an airplane multiple times a week and living off of fast food was a recipe for obesity. Seeing these living harbingers, he had determined to live a more active and disciplined lifestyle, which included walking or biking whenever possible, never using the hotel elevator (even with a carry-on bag) and eating at any restaurant except fast food joints.

Because of these personal precepts, he had been able to experience the towns he visited in a way that left positive memories, even if they were less metropolitan or downright rural. *Everywhere has something to offer,* he often reminded himself.

He had finished his cold calls and visits for the day and really had a craving for sushi. He first walked into a place with a rusty sign above the sagging awning that said Mike's Seafood – Oysters, Crab Legs and Lobster. A dour faced teenage girl was slumped behind the hostess stand as he entered. She reluctantly quit scrolling on her smartphone and asked, "Just one?"

"Yes, please," he replied with a bright smile.

She turned and walked away saying, "Let me wipe down

a table for you." He barely heard her retreating words. His optimism held fast until he saw the health rating, which had 82 written across it in big red letters. He squinted as he read the comments in the dim setting: raw food on counters, freezer not at required temperature, Band-Aid observed on floor.

Check please!, he thought as he visualized the kitchen where his food would be prepared. The teenager returned, dirty dishrag in hand, just in time to hear the bell on the door ring as their only patron had made his escape.

Feeling grateful to have avoided an appointment with salmonella, he noticed a local grocery store ahead with a flashing sign that proudly boasted, "Best Seafood in Richfield. Free Show! (Afternoons from 3:00 PM to 7:00 PM)." He, like anyone, thought this was odd, but the marketing worked as intended. He crossed the parking lot, walked through the automatic sliding doors and made his way to the back of the store.

He was both doubtful and curious as he neared the rear area where large "MEAT" and "SEAFOOD" lettering was mounted high on the walls. He raised an eyebrow as he noticed that glitter paint had been added to the latter. Rounding one last corner, he stopped in his tracks as he observed approximately twenty people huddled around the counter and glass display cases. To get a better view, a father was hoisting his small son onto his shoulders, wonder and awe obvious in his young eyes. Like a reporter trying to get the attention of a celebrity, he squeezed through the outer ranks and craned his head to see what all the fuss was about.

There behind the counter were two people that were about a dissimilar as any he'd ever seen. Although they were both adorned in matching white chef hats and shirts, the man was obviously Asian, stocky with hard eyes. His dark goatee fell downward like a short waterfall. To his left, looking miniscule proportionally was a typical teenage girl, pretty but unusually natural in appearance. He wondered if the store had some policy against makeup or jewelry.

They worked in silence, yet their synchronization was amazing. Their eyes were trained on the cutting surface below and yet their hands were tossing and catching knives and slabs of fish, which flew between them like some dangerous juggling act. Without warning, one would toss a blade, which would flip in the air toward the other. A hand would shoot out like a viper, retrieving the blade that would swing downward with dazzling quickness. Filets would split perfectly in half and be wrapped in butcher paper almost faster than the eye could perceive. The audience oohed and aahed quietly, but not loud enough to interrupt the almost sacred display of fish mongering.

The guy looks the part, but where did they find this girl? he asked himself. Like other customers, he pulled his smart phone from his pocket and began filming.

Simmons Lane, Richfield

As the sun began to set, Mandy and Helly walked down the quiet sidewalk through their neighborhood. Little Maddie rode contently in her stroller. It had become a time for the two women, who'd become close friends, to talk and tell each other about their day.

"So, how is work going?" Mandy asked.

"It is very fulfilling. Chores were a daily part of life in the monastery so this responsibility makes me feel more at home."

Mandy reflected on how mature and unusual that sounded coming from a teenager. "Are you not intimidated by Chun?"

Helly looked puzzled.

"What I mean is that he looks intimidating: big guy, goatee, angry expression. It looks like he might stab a customer in the heart if they complained," she said with a laugh.

Helly frowned as she asked, "Is this an acceptable response to a complaint?"

Suddenly becoming serious, Mandy answered. "No, no, no. I was just being silly. Unfortunately, Americans are famous for their complaining. I suppose being able to complain is what makes America great. If we hadn't complained, we might be serving the King of England today. However, fast food burgers still look nothing like the pictures on the menu. I guess you have to pick your battles."

"Is this an American expression?"

"Pick your battles? I guess so. You typically use it when talking about teenagers. Some things they do need to be discussed heavily and discouraged. Other things probably aren't worth the fight."

"Do you speak of this from experience? Have I been difficult?"

"Heavens, no!" Mandy stopped and turned to position herself directly in front of Helly. "Helly, Tom and I believe you came to us for a reason. We don't believe in chance or coincidence. You are such a big help around the house and with Maddie...and we like you. We keep expecting a rebellious attitude to surface or some type of bad behavior, but they haven't. You are special, Helly. Special to us. Special to God."

As usual, Helly digested these words with a silence that would make one wonder if she'd heard them at all. It made the moment a little awkward, so Mandy decided to go on the offensive. She slowly lifted her right hand, placed it behind Helly's left shoulder and gently pulled her into a hug. Helly allowed herself to be drawn in and awkwardly tried to reciprocate the gesture. As she placed her hands on Mandy's back, she felt that strange sensation again. It was like realizing how thirsty you actually were on a hot day. It was like the welcoming warmth of a fire on a winter's day.

Master Quon's Karate Dojo, Richfield

Hebruce was in full effect. Upon arriving, he had excused himself and stepped into what appeared to be a closet. As Helly waited, she looked at the myriad of trophies and photos displayed on every wall. A recent one showed Hebruce bowing before his sensei, who was reverently presenting a brown belt to his student. At that moment, he exited the changing room dressed in a karategi, which is the traditional uniform. Many Americans simply referred to the white cotton garment as a gi (pronounced ghee). His brown belt was cinched tightly around his waist. Helly frowned as she examined the large padded gloves, shin guards and helmet he was also adorned with. His normally whimsical face was now masked with a serious expression that was all business.

Without speaking, he walked to a nearby rack of equipment and retrieved another set of pads. As he offered them to her, she asked, "What is the purpose of the armor?"

He acted like the answer should be obvious. "To keep you from getting hurt, duuuuhhhh."

Helly thought before speaking. "My teachers explained that shielding limits one's mobility. The balance of the two must be firmly decided upon by the warrior before entering battle."

"Are you saying you don't want 'em?" He leaned in and lowered his voice. "Look. I'm not about hitting girls but, on the mat, everyone is equal. You never know who you're going to run into out there on the streets, so we train like we fight."

Helly replied, "That sounds familiar." She removed her shoes, as instructed, before stepping on the mat. Wearing white socks, blue jeans and a light blue t-shirt, she watched inquisitively as Hebruce began to prowl around the perimeter of the pads.

He walked as if moving through thick water, each step like the delayed gait of a tiger. As he moved, he rolled his shoulders and threw faint punches with each hand at some invisible adversary. Finally, he turned, faced Helly and bowed. She understood enough to return the signal.

"Alright, I'm going to take it easy on you since you're...well, you know." With that, he ducked his head slightly and began to approach with his hands held open about chest height. Helly stood motionless as he drew near. Suddenly, he spun in a circle. "HeeYAH!" he yelled as his right leg left the ground and swung around like a hammer through the air. However, he spun out of control and almost fell over when his foot failed to connect with anything. Steadying himself, he looked at his opponent, who was somehow standing just beyond what should have been the path of destruction. He immediately regrouped and lunged forward, hoping to grab the collar of her shirt and take her down to the mat. He felt quick impacts on his forearms as his momentum increased. He sprawled out face first and slid onto the wooden floor beyond the pads.

Helly turned and watched him roll over and kip onto his feet. Angrily, he assumed a full attack position and let out a battle cry. "YeAHHHHHHH!!!" There was a fire in his eyes that reflected embarrassment and anger. He ran at her, leaping high off the ground while extending his right foot toward her sternum. The impact could have broken a rib. However, there was no impact, at least not with a human target. Once again, Hebruce found his momentum accelerated unnaturally. He flew high, near the ceiling tiles, as he flapped his arms like an ungainly bird. This time, he landed on the floor and then collided with the wall. Trophies toppled and a framed photo fell to the floor. The sound of glass cracking was ignored.

If anything, he was resilient. Now full of fury, he marched directly toward her and began to throw wild punches toward her face and torso. Like an optical illusion, her body somehow seemed to disappear from where it had been a split second before. Throughout the visually vicious attack, he observed that she looked bored. After three more attempts, he dropped his arms, sweat appearing on his forehead and ragged breaths escaping from his lungs. He looked down at his belt as if he'd forgotten to press an "on" button.

"I...don't...understand," he panted.

Helly felt more awkward than at any other time since she'd arrived in the States. She was more than an excellent judge of character. She was a veritable expert at assessing threats. Sadly, Hebruce was not included in this hallowed ranking. She also understood from her time with the male trainees at the monastery that a certain pride existed among men that could not be peeled away. It flowed through their veins and was revealed in their eyes. With some exceptions, they knew they were the stronger sex: larger, faster, more aggressive. However, it had been their physical advantages that had helped to forge her into what she now was. Her adaptation had been a necessity. Here, standing before a humiliated warrior, she pondered this new dynamic with the opposite gender. He was a male, but he was also her friend – a harmless, brown belted friend.

Pity was not shown towards opponents, so Helly bowed respectfully, walked off the mat and began to put on her shoes.

Burgerzone, Richfield

They sat on opposite sides of a booth facing each other. Samantha was shoving fries in her mouth with one hand between sips of her strawberry milkshake. Helly sat ramrod straight as she examined the grease that saturated the paper below her meal.

"Do you think I should call him?" Samantha's face was contorted with indecision.

"Call who?"

"Cody. My boyfriend?"

Helly sat silently. She had never participated in consoling or girl talk.

Samantha continued. "You know, it wasn't all bad. He took me out and we would watch movies." She looked down at the table. "He would kiss me." She paused. "It's just that, now I'm alone again. And who knows when someone else will come along. It's so unfair that guys get to ask out anybody they want to and girls just have to sit around, primping and hoping to be picked. Ever played a game where they are picking teams and you just sit there as everyone else gets chosen? That's how I feel." With that, she crossed her arms over her chest and dismally slumped against the seatback.

Helly contemplated what her friend was saying. No, she had never been part of a team sport and had certainly never dated. She perceived that her friend was asking her for advice and yet, she understood that she had no experience to qualify her to offer any.

"Perhaps there is someone else in your life that could be of assistance to you right now."

Samantha frowned heavily. Thankfully, she was mindful that Helly did not understand Western culture and courtesies. Otherwise, her statement would have been even more hurtful.

"You're my bestie! You're supposed to tell me that Cody is a creep and that I'd be loser to go back to him. We're supposed to trash him and talk about what a jerk he is until we run out of bad things to say, and then you're supposed to reassure me that I have a lot to offer and that someone who appreciates me will come along."

Helly processed this information and nodded slowly. "I understand."

A moment of silence passed between them before Helly spoke again. "I assume that this term 'bestie' implies that I have an important role in your social circle. I assume that this position includes responsibilities and expectations."

"It's usually not that formal but, yeah."

"Forgive me if I do not include the necessary slang but Cody is completely self-serving in his pursuit of you. It is in his character to only take and never to serve." Helly formulated her thoughts. "Although I have not experienced a romantic relationship, I have observed Tom and Mandy. Their interactions with each other are starkly differently than those you have described with Cody. Tom is very delicate with Mandy. He is not effeminate, but he measures his actions and words as if he were handling a valuable vase. I see him opening her door, carrying her bags, and caressing her with his touch. This is not common among his male friends. They are more like, how do you say, cave people."

"You mean cavemen."

"Yes. Cavemen. They vigorously engage in sports, slap each other in various places and say crude things to each other. It is more akin to your relationship."

Samantha sunk further into her seat. "Not helping," she said.

"What I am saying is that you are more like a Mandy than a male companion. And Mandys do well to have a Tom."

"But that's so old fashioned. Guys don't do that stuff anymore. They aren't gallant. They aren't selfless. They just want some eye candy and to make out."

"I assume these are objectifying and sensual terms."

"YES!" Samantha was really purging her emotions. "Why do I want what I know is bad for me? Am I going to be one of those women bouncing around from loser to loser just because she is afraid of being alone?"

Helly listened silently and attentively.

"How do you do it?"

"I do not understand what you are referring to."

"Being alone. You have me and, I guess, you have Hebruce. You sort of have a family with the Masons but, otherwise, you are alone. You have been alone. And it doesn't seem to bother you. You seem like you'd be fine on some deserted island for the rest of your life."

Helly remained silent as she considered this. Had she been more familiar with American mannerisms, she would have understood this to be venting.

Samantha realized that her words could be construed as hurtful so she slid out of her seat and slid in beside Helly.

Laying her head on her friend's shoulder, she lamented, "What are we gonna do? We are seventeen, we're beautiful and we're doomed to be old maids."

The Mason's Home,
Simmons Dr. Richfield

After completing her shift at Buckston's, Helly was expecting another routine evening with the Masons. A meal and their company would have been more than sufficient for her expectations. It was normal for her to clean up and enter through their back door without the necessity of knocking. Tonight, however, she was surprised. Pushing open the door, she saw Tom sliding on his jacket and Mandy tugging one onto little Maddie as well.

"Good evening. It would appear that our dinner plans are being altered."

"You can say that again," Tom replied with a goofy grin on his face.

Helly looked to Mandy for clarification. "The fair is in town. Tom thought it would be a great idea for you and Maddie to experience it."

"I assume by your use of "it," the fair is not a person."

"What?" Tom exclaimed. "You've never been to the fair?" His question might have been hurtful if it had not been laden with so much glee and a goofy expression. "It's the world's best show in town!" His gibberish made absolutely no sense to Helly, but the mood was infectious. Instantly, she was curious and excited to acquaint herself with this mysterious fair.

They loaded up into the minivan with Tom and Mandy performing a fun duet along with Sonny and Cher. Helly observed Maddie bobbing her head and trying to mimic the words even as she was confined to her car seat. In a moment, she experimented with the movement of her head. At first, it was just a simple nod in time with the rhythm. Then, it evolved into a tilt from side to side, and then into a serpentine wiggle that extended down to her shoulders. Mandy caught this out of her peripheral vision and smiled.

As they neared their turn, the traffic became congested. Maddie began to crane her neck as she investigated the nearby electric glow that lit up a fourth of the horizon. Helly had never seen anything like it. As the doors opened, the unmistakable scent of corn dogs and funnel cakes filled their noses. Tom paid their admission and Helly stared at the smear of ink that had been stamped on the back of her hand.

"It lets everyone know you didn't sneak in," Tom explained. This gave her the sensation of having an exclusive membership. This was not a low-class affair. Apparently, Tom and Mandy had connections, or at least more clout that she had realized.

"So, we should not encounter any riffraff inside of this event."

Tom looked puzzled. "I'm sorry, Helly, but why do you ask?"

Looking admiringly at her stamp, she explained. "I was told about elite circles in society. Never in my most undomesticated dreams did I envision such prestigious inclusion."

Mandy replied, "Honey, I think you mean your 'wildest dreams.' Actually, the fair is not that prestigious. It only costs five dollars to get in the gate."

Tom spoke up. "Yeah. The corndogs are where they

really get you. We'll probably drop fifty bucks on food tonight." Mandy cut her eyes at him, causing him to add, "Which is gonna be totally worth it!"

Mandy and Maddie rode the kiddie rides. Squeals and smiles abounded. The four took selfies and laughed as they stood in front of the wavy mirrors. Looking very much like a giraffe in one of the reflections, Helly put her hands on her head and tried to push it back down into place.

"Helly, is there a ride you want to check out?"

She had been eyeing the Ferris wheel ever since they'd arrived. The wonder of its illuminated circumference reflected in her blue eyes. Lifting her hand, she pointed.

Mandy and Maddie watched as Tom and Helly took their seat and had the single safety bar locked into place. As the ride operator completed the task, Helly said aloud, "It appears that riffraff are welcome at the fair."

Tom's face turned red as the carnie glared at her. Embarrassed and caught in the spotlight, Tom pointed to Helly and mouthed an apologetic, "Foreign exchange student." Thankfully, the carnie accepted this and moved on.

As the wheel started and they began to ascend, Tom watched as fascination overwhelmed his riding partner. He thought back to his childhood when everything was new and wonderous. Sure, he was able to experience this with Maddie to some degree, but seeing it in a young adult allowed for feedback.

"Helly, will you share your thoughts out loud?"

She thought for a moment and spoke. "I feel as if I am in a dream. The stories I heard about America were always tainted by cautionary tales and warnings. Now, to experience this, I feel as if I am among the most fortunate people in the world."

Tom digested this and thought to himself, *and this is just the Ferris wheel.*

Their contemplation came crashing to a halt as a loud clang was heard in the next seat ahead. Apparently, some bolt or mechanism had failed, causing it to tilt wildly. They were at the apex of the ride and its occupants let out blood curdling screams as they began to dangle fifty feet above the ground. One of the riders had slipped underneath the safety bar. His friend had grabbed his shirt collar, which was now tearing quickly.

Tom pointed and shouted to no one in particular. "He's going to fall!"

Onlookers from below took notice and only added to the bedlam with their collective yelling. The carnie yanked at the control lever, which caused the wheel to lurch to a stop. This only added to the seat's swinging, causing it to drop several more inches. Tom felt completely helpless. That's when he noticed that the space beside him was vacant. Panic seized his chest as he whipped his head around to find Helly.

Perched atop the thin framework of the ancient ride, there she was, walking forward with the smoothness of a cat. Tom tried to speak and demand that she return, but the words caught in his throat. He simply sat with one hand outstretched toward her and the other gripping the safety bar. He watched in terror as she easily crossed the span, slid down the support beams and took hold of the dangling passenger. Pulling him close, the boy was able to latch onto the metal lattice and find secure footing. Helly moved like a spider in a web as she moved toward the next seat and guided the young boy's foot and hand placement.

When they arrived, its occupants gladly accepted their terrified guest. Then, they received a peculiar yet friendly wave from Helly, who disappeared behind them. Tom watched open mounted as she lithely climbed back up the framework, traversed the railing like a trapeze artist and slid back into their seat. Horrified, he could only stare at her. She looked at him and announced, "I think I would like to try the cake of the funnel next."

Hebruce Lee's Home,
520 Pinheel Drive, Richfield

It had been five days since their duel at the dojo. Hebruce had disappeared and could not be found. Helly understood his reasons but she also needed his help. More importantly, he comprised 50% of her pie plate of teenage friends. She stood on his front porch and knocked three times on the door. Apparently, someone inside could see her because she heard a woman's voice.

"Bruce! One of your little friends is at the door. It's a girl!"

Moments went by before she heard footsteps approaching from inside and the door slowly opened. Hebruce looked terrible. The spark of life had drained from his countenance. Without making eye contact, he glumly greeted her. "Hi, Helly. What do you want?"

"I am concerned about you. You have not spoken to me since our visit to your dojo. There is no reason for this."

"Yes, there is!" His voice was tinged with anger. "You're a girl. I was supposed to win...easily. I've been taking karate lessons for almost four years. I really thought I was becoming something, but you've shown me that it's all been a waste of time. I'm nothing but a poser-wannabe."

"I am not familiar with this 'poser-wannabe.' The words I would have chosen include show-boater and braggart. These may be outdated in today's vernacular."

He was done with this conversation. He began to shut

the door. Right before it closed, a hand shot through the opening and took hold of his collar. Her foot was now wedged in the gap. He did not want to be embarrassed again in his own home, so he reopened the door and pulled her inside.

Once he closed the door, he quietly hissed, "Would you cut that out! That's what I'm talking about. You can't be superior to me. It's not natural!"

Helly listened without judgment. Silence ensued until he continued.

"Look, Helly. You are an amazing girl. I'm just gonna throw this out there and let it land wherever. You are beautiful without any help. You're mature and wise and poised. It's like some adult got trapped inside of a teenager. I can't decide if you're like a friend or a mom. And the one thing that I thought I had on you, I don't."

He went just a little further. "I'm a guy and I really like spending time with you, but you make it hard for me to feel like a guy. Does this make any sense?"

Helly nodded and thought back to her conversation with Samantha. "There are many things about Western culture and relationships that I do not understand. For example, I am not sure if I'm expected to show you sympathy at this moment or to correct you for showing weakness. Either seems detrimental to the veneer of ego that I've observed in young American men." Her tone was neutral but intentional.

"Maybe you're right. Maybe we are a bunch of babies acting like grown-ups, but would your teachers have ever brought a girl flowers? Would they ever write a song for them? Would they ever act like a fool just to make you smile?"

Helly couldn't help but to contrast these acts with those of Samantha's suitor.

He continued his rant, "You know, Americans may not be perfect, but we have a lot going for us. I don't see people sneaking over the border into China."

She nodded. "You make an excellent point. Toupée."

"I think you mean 'touché.'"

The tension ebbed as he regathered himself. She broke the silence. "Your technical proficiency is evident. It is merely your attitude and motivation."

"What?"

"Your karate. You have the foundation to be a respectable warrior. You only lack the refinement."

He shook his head and smiled before confessing. "You know, Helly. You're a real straight shooter. I think that's what I like about you the most."

John Cleveland

PART III

三

John Cleveland

Byerton University Campus

It's a proven fact that attractive people have an advantage. They get hired over others, get paid more and are typically chosen first. It isn't fair, but the fairest among us aren't complaining. As Matthew accelerated away from the campus bookstore in his red Mustang convertible, he unconsciously checked himself out in the rearview mirror: tanned skin, bright white teeth and strong facial features. Satisfied with what he saw, he turned his eyes back to the road.

Born into an affluent family, life had been comparatively easy for him. Even as a child, he learned that charm and cuteness could get you out of a whole lot of trouble. That, of course, led to a pattern of perpetual trouble. Perhaps much of the blame fell onto his parents. Discipline was not high on their list of priorities. His dad was of the opinion that if you provided well for your family, you had satisfied all of your requirements as a father. Hence, any deficiencies in his role as a mentor were camouflaged with lavish vacations, the newest toy or an inground swimming pool.

His mom was quite happy with the arrangement. They decided to have a child because, well, that's what you do. After Matthew was born, her focus was on returning to her pre-pregnancy size. There were endless hours at the gym, including dozens of sessions with a personal trainer.

Thankfully, Fit-Quest offered childcare. Also, they wanted to protect their posterity and hopefully have someone to look after them in their old age. They viewed their last will and testament as an insurance policy to ensure that this would happen. As Matthew was beginning his independence, they often reminded him of his family obligations and that his future endowment was conditional. Ever the rebel, he wanted a Plan B. Although he felt little admiration, he would follow in his father's footsteps. He would climb the ladder, he would take the road less traveled, and he would become a self-made man. Armed with his dad's credit card, a generous monthly allowance and low expectations, he had ample time to scheme.

Like most other guys his age, girls tended to board his train of thought about once every ten seconds. Cutting his eyes toward two cute coeds jogging down the sidewalk, he momentarily drifted across the center line before a car horn reminded him to pay more attention to the road. He proactively strategized how he would happen to bump into them, what he would say, all the while looking very earnest and trustworthy. Picking up girls, like all things in his world, had become too easy. The clothes, the smile, the car, the hair – he had the whole package.

Now in his third year of college, he was itching to reach a higher level. Very much like a drug addiction, he found that it took more and more conquests to feel any sense of satisfaction. When it came to popularity and prosperity, he was already in the top tenth percentile. However, that seemed so mediocre knowing that some elite circle was solidly in the top one percent. As these thoughts subconsciously tumbled through his mind, he thought to himself, *I think I'll swing by the gym and hop in the tanning bed for a while. There's always hot chicks at the gym.*

The Mason's Home,
Simmons Lane, Richfield

Dinner was later than usual tonight. Helly had been asked by her manager to work an hour over to keep up with the increased demand for seafood orders. Fortunately for the Masons, that resulted in an order placed by a customer that was never picked up. Pecan crusted salmon tonight! The plates were served and everyone took their seats as Tom thanked God for the day that was now winding down.

"So how did work go today?" Tom asked Helly.

"It was very fulfilling. I have been awarded a raise of fifty cents per hour due to the increase in our department's productivity."

Smile were exchanged with "Congratulations!" from Mandy and Tom. Even Maddie seemed to recognize that something was being celebrated.

"Helly, we are so very proud of you. You are making friends, making our lives easier around the house and doing so well at your job," Tom said.

Helly was learning to accept accolades. "Thank you," she said with a slight bow of her head.

"So, what's the happy hap?" he asked, a big grin on his face.

Helly looked puzzled, so Mandy filled in. "It was a popular expression when we were your age. He was just asking what events are new in your life, I mean, what's been going on." Mandy had found herself slipping into the same robotic language that Helly used as she tried to explain Western culture.

"Samantha is deliberating if she should return to her brutish boyfriend, Cody. Hebruce is experiencing embarrassment because he was unable to assault me at the dojo." This elicited brief looks of concern between Tom and Mandy. "And I am entertaining the idea of attending an American college next year." Eyes widened at her news.

Tom cautiously replied. "I want to, uh, revisit the assault at the dojo but, first, tell me about this whole college thing. We hadn't even thought about that for some reason."

"Samantha is planning to attend Byerton University after graduating next spring. Her parents studied at this institution which was also the location of their courting and engagement."

Nods ensued. "Byerton's great! I would have loved to have gone there if we could have afforded it," Mandy said. "Maybe you could get a scholarship because you're, um...Asian." Even as she said it, it felt awkward and somehow not wholly accurate. She bit her lip, wishing she could suck it back in. Thankfully, the opportunity for offense passed over Helly. "What I mean is that minorities often qualify for tuition assistance..."

Tom rescued her from the quicksand. "I think what Mandy is trying to say is that you would be a good candidate for Byerton. You're smart, athletic, hardworking and likeable."

More accolades. "Thank you for the encouragement, Tom."

There was a moment of awkward silence, which Tom broke with another question. "So, tell me about this assault business."

Master Quon's Karate Dojo, Richfield

Helly was required to sign a release of liability when she returned with Hebruce to the dojo. Fresh paint covered a recently repaired indention in the sheetrock and a framed photo on one of the shelves now had tape reinforcing its edges.

She was wearing a borrowed karategi and stood barefoot on the blue pads. Hebruce meekly offered her a set of protective pads, which she refused by simply not acknowledging them. They stood about eight feet apart and bowed to each other before she spoke.

"I believe the expression in English is telegraphing. Are you familiar with this?"

With a shrug, he replied, "Sure. It's when you do something that lets your opponent know you're about to try something sneaky."

"Correct. However, the act of telegraphing occurs well before the actual confrontation. I have seen my male counterparts signaling their desire to fight by expanding their chest, flaring their arms outward and scowling. Perhaps it cannot be helped but it is not beneficial. Revealing your intention or capability gives your enemy a tremendous advantage."

Hebruce nodded, absorbing this knowledge from someone he knew to be knowledgeable.

"If the use of deception is advantageous, one may actually want to appear weak, unprepared or even ill-

215

equipped."

"Not the American way, but, whatever."

"You will notice, I have not assumed a fighting stance or expressed aggression with my face. How do you interpret this?"

"I'm not sure. The first time, I thought you were an easy target but, now, not so much."

"Very good. You are learning. Now, why did you initiate an attack the last time we were here?"

That's a great question, he thought as he pondered how to answer. There was no sense in lying to someone who always seemed to be three steps ahead of him intellectually. "I was showing off. I wanted to impress you."

"I am learning that this is common in the Western culture. However, you would benefit from being less assuming and better prepared. They actually go hair in hair."

"I think you mean 'hand in hand.'"

"Yes. Hand in hand. Do you understand?"

"Less assuming but better prepared. But why take all these lessons if you're never going to use them? There are some jerks out there that really need their butts kicked."

She considered this. "Yes, but let them be the ones who create the opportunity. Do not let this be you." Helly paused before she asked, "Do you currently feel threatened?"

"No. Not really. We're just kinda' talking."

With that, she turned and slowly walked away toward the edge of the mat as if she were leaving. Then, without warning, she spun toward him, let out an ear-piercing scream and charged at him. She closed the gap in less than two seconds. He flinched, yelped aloud and shrank into a cowardly posture. She tackled him, knocking the wind out of him as they slid off of the opposite side. She hopped up and returned to her previous spot.

Struggling to sit up, he slowly asked, "What – was – that?!?"

"It was a test of your mindset. Had you not considered this as a possibility?"

"You bowling me over like a crazy person?!? No!" He was dusting himself off as he stood up.

"Your awareness of the situation must expand to all possibilities, at all times. Passivity is the greatest detriment to preparedness."

"That seems crazy. Are you saying that even as you hang out with the Masons, eating dinner at their table, that you are expecting Tom to throw a steak knife at you?"

"I am, but I am also expecting good things from Tom, like kind words, questions about my life and more potatoes."

He wasn't sure if she was being funny or if this was just more of her language snafus. "I'm not sure I could go through life being on edge like that. I mean, don't you ever wish you could just turn it off?"

Helly thought about this to the point that her eyes deviated away from Hebruce down toward the mat. Finally, with a noticeably weaker voice, she replied, "I'm not sure I know how." She shook her head and returned to the lesson. "Now, to become proficient in combat, one must AYYYYEEEEE!!!!"

Her scream once more resonated throughout the dojo as she lunged at him but, this time, he reacted. Instinctively, he kicked his hips to the right, braced himself with his right leg and shoved her with his hands as she passed by. She regained her footing, turned and smiled. "Very good."

Byerton University Campus

Matthew was brainstorming. *Think! How can I reach the financial status of my dad so that I don't need him anymore?* It's an odd arrangement to resent the person that's paying your tuition...and your rent...and your grocery bill...and everything else. Even though he had a cool car (with no car payment) and the ability to buy almost anything he wanted, he knew he was still a "dependent." The word made him sick and angry, like a child that is trying to express what it wants but hasn't yet learned how to speak.

Get a job? No. It would interfere with my social life. Lottery tickets? Astronomically low chance of winning, a fool's errand. Crime? Guys like me don't do well in prison. Think, Matthew, THINK!!!

Frustration was building up inside like a carbonated soda. He had to get outside, burn some energy, get somewhere where he could think. He left his apartment and walked the block to where the campus started. He walked through the brick and concrete archway that proudly declared "Byerton University, est. 1941, Home of the Beavers, 1977 State Champions." It always felt nice to be here, sort of like a mini utopia. Everyone was young and most were attractive. It was always clean, the grass was always manicured and security kept out all the riffraff.

He had his hands in his pockets and was looking down at the sidewalk as he ambled aimlessly. Suddenly, he heard his name being called.

"Hey, Matt!" It was a guy's voice, nasally and familiar. Any voice besides a female's failed to excite him. He looked up and realized that he was passing by the science building. There, on the steps, was Harmon Green. Matthew audibly moaned and then exhaled at the sight of him. He and Harmon had gone to high school together and now Harmon mistakenly thought that it made them friends.

Matthew had an image to maintain and his "cool ranking" could be deeply affected by even being seen with a dork like Harmon. He had always been a brainiac. You know, one of those guys whose hand shoots up before the teacher even finishes the question, the kind that wiggles in his seat until he is called. *I thought people quit doing that in second grade,* Matthew thought as he recalled his childhood.

Matthew changed direction and acted as if he hadn't heard the call, but it was too late. He could hear Harmon's steps quickly approaching from behind as he yelled out again. "Matt! It's me, Harmon! Wait up, buddy!" Matthew shrunk down, wishing he could crawl under the grass. With few options, he turned around.

"Whaddaya want, Harmon?" Matthew blandly asked.

"Hey, man. Haven't seen you much since Richfield High. What's been going on?" Harmon's demeanor was light and upbeat, almost desperate.

"Nothin' much. Just school and stuff."

"Come on, man! I know you've been doing more than studying. You've always been good with the ladies." He grinned and casually tapped Matthew on the shoulder. Matthew disgustedly looked down at his sleeve as if someone has just smeared oil on his expensive shirt. "What I mean is that, you know, everyone knows you have a way with girls that not all of us do."

Matthew raised an eyebrow. He wasn't sure where this was going.

Harmon looked down and fumbled with his hands as he tried to decide how to proceed. He then looked up and declared somewhat triumphantly, "I've discovered something."

Both eyebrows were now raised. Could it really be this easy? He had been brainstorming about how to make some real money and cut his apron strings when this nerd singles him out with some great idea.

"Discovered what?"

Harmon looked around to make sure no one was within earshot. "It happened by accident. I was thinking about a product that, if invented, could revolutionize study habits. 84% of college students and 92% of high school students admit to having a lack or even an absence of motivation when it comes to studying!" He was obviously excited about this information. Matthew rolled his eyes as this small bubble of hope popped. "So, I began to research the chemical pathways in our brains that cause us to make excuses, see things as favorable, or analyze the work-to-reward factors of endeavors."

"You've lost me."

"Wanting vs. not-wanting! Don't you see? Humans have a proclivity for talking themselves out of things even if they include potential benefits. 'I'm not going to apply for that job. I'm not qualified. I'm not going to ask her out. She'll probably say no. I'm not going out this weekend. It's easier to stay at home.'"

"I still don't get what you're talking about."

Harmon was mildly exasperated but continued. "Students have to study to make good grades, but few want to. What if there was a drug that you could take that would convince your mind that studying was fun or entertaining, or at least rewarding? What if you could take a pill and all of your excuses disappeared? What if you could instantly rewire your mind to be agreeable to something that previously sounded awful?"

Matthew was imaging this but still failed to see any value in wanting to study, or even studying for that matter. "Look, Harmon. Congratulations. You seem like the kind of guy that could easily get hired by some pharmaceutical company. Good luck." Matthew turned and was about to walk away when he felt a hand on his arm. He spun, his eyes instantly filled with anger. He had let the first touch go, but no one was allowed to grab Matthew Winston and live.

Harmon's eyes were now pleading. "There was a problem. It's something that I can't fix. I need the help of someone more like you."

Matthew interpreted this as an insinuation that he was a bonehead and the opposite of a brainiac like Harmon. He clenched his fists and was weighing his options.

"I identified the proteins which affect motivation and developed a catalyst that activates the specific synthesis but..."

Matthew waited, poised to punch if this got any weirder.

"But the only catalyst that I've identified is alcohol."

Matthew unclenched his fists. Maybe there was some need for his field of expertise. He still had not connected all the dots. "So, how does this involve me?"

Harmon relaxed, seeing that he finally had Matthew's interest. "Well, obviously studying and drinking don't go well together. I thought about scrapping the whole project until you came to mind."

A handsome eyebrow was raised once more.

"In high school, you were always one of the preps or jocks or whatever you want to call them. You were popular. You went to parties. You could have any girl you wanted. Guys like me saw you as some sort of demigod, as if your mom had hooked up with Zeus. You had the whole package. You lived in a world that we could only dream of."

Matthew shrugged off his acknowledgement of this fact.

"When the concept of a willingness drug suddenly required alcohol, I had a thought. *Could I use this to my advantage with girls?*"

The pieces were now starting to fit. Harmon didn't need a guinea pig. He needed a wingman. The wheels in Matthew's sinister mind began to turn. *How many nerds would pay big bucks to have some hottie suddenly be into them?* He could be the gateway, albeit at a hefty fee. This could be it. This could be his golden ticket. Harmon would provide the drugs and he would provide the introduction.

As natural as a chameleon, Matthew smiled warmly at his new business partner and put an arm around his shoulder. Harmon reveled in the gesture of acceptance.

With an amazing blend of slyness and sincerity, Matthew said, "You came to right man, buddy. I think I can help you out."

Buckston's Grocery, Richfield

Other departments were starting to experience some disparity. The produce lead grumbled that his lettuce display was "lackluster." The beverage lead reported that several brands of soda were out of stock on his shelves. The florist lamented that the lilies were wilting. When the associates had complained to Charlie, his reply was the same. "When you get your numbers up like Seafood, we'll reallocate more of the budget for your department." Even though neither Chun nor Helly had ever done anything to be resented by their co-workers, they were now secretly and scornfully referred to as the "Tuna Twins."

New signs had been erected near the entrance which displayed "See Your Seafood Prepared, Daily From 3:00 PM to 7:00 PM." Arrows cleverly shaped like fish were adhered to the floor and pointed customers toward the back of the store. Management had also spent a small fortune buying new display cases, which were lower to the ground so that larger audiences could have a better view. Separating the newly enlarged wooden cutting surface was a large panel of plexiglass, for liability reasons.

A dramatic backdrop had been erected which boasted "WARNING!!! Professional Food Preparation in Progress. Surgically Sharp Blades in Use." Images of samurai swords slicing through filets of fish, which were falling towards waiting plates below accompanied the shameless promotional message. Multi-colored spotlights shown down on the work area.

Chun and Helly understood that they were now providing entertainment as well as food services, but they had little reason to complain. Money is definitely a morale booster, but their fulfillment came from being appreciated. At an even deeper level, they enjoyed being excellent. Their skill had been developed over decades (1.7 decades in Helly's case) and it was finally being put to good use. At Charlie's requests, they now stood further apart so that the airtime of the blades increased. He thought the extra three feet added flair to their exhibition. It's a good thing he didn't realize they would still be comfortable exchanging knives at thirty feet.

Helly had learned that Chun was the son of immigrants who came to the States in the late 1990s. His family had fished the waters of the East China Sea for generations. He had actually been born on the fishing boat where his parents lived and worked. Whereas American children grew up riding bicycles and playing baseball, his earliest memories were of nets and hooks. He was ten years old when his family defected to South Korea and eventually made their way to America. However, the saltwater was already in his veins. Try as he may, no other profession ever seemed to be a good fit. After years of floundering as an insurance salesman, taxi driver and an extremely brief stint as a dental hygienist, he finally found his way behind a cutting board and fell into his groove. There wasn't much he could do about his stocky build, but the goatee and intimidating persona were actually just barriers to keep people at arm's length. Isolation is the ally of introverts.

Nevertheless, he had come to deeply care for Helly. To be able to speak in his native language had been like a pressure valve being released. To find someone who appreciated proficiency and a sharp blade was more than endearing. These attributes and benefits had stirred an inclination within him to watch over her and protect her. However, he also sensed that it was not necessary.

Maple Ridge Greenway

Helly and Samantha walked along the now leaf laden path. Vivid yellows stood out brightly amongst the wall of orange and red leaves on either side. They wore light coats and their breaths had been visible earlier that morning.

Samantha was still pining about the perfect man. "First of all, he needs to be a gentleman. No burping, no farting and preferably no bad language. He can be a sports fan, but not one of those glued-to-the-TV-every-Sunday guys. He needs to be a good conversationalist, a good listener. He needs to be patient and understanding when my mood is all over the place. He needs to be nice to his mother..."

Helly was listening and wondering if this list of qualifications was unique to Samantha or if most girls had a similar set of criteria.

"As far as looks, he needs to be handsome but not a pretty boy. Plenty enough for me, but not so much that he's always getting checked out by other girls."

Helly hadn't given much thought to a partner. Surrounded exclusively by men and boys for most of her life, she felt more male than female in many regards. She was not emotional. She felt no butterflies in her stomach around boys. She felt no need for protection or provision. If anything, they existed in her mind as associates. Everyone had a job to do and she would take her place alongside her fellow coworkers in this responsibility known as life, simple as that.

"How about you? What's your dream guy like?"

Helly stopped walking and thought before answering. "Is it mandatory that women are to be married in this country?"

"No, but most people do. Well, at least they used to."

"What are the benefits of being married versus not being married?"

It was Samantha's turn to think. "I'm not entirely sure. I guess if you're NOT married, you can do what you want when you want. You don't have to worry about him cheating on you or ever going through a divorce. You're not stuck with the same guy until you die." She paused, "But you are alone. Even if you're dating someone, there's no real commitment there. They can walk away whenever they please. What about when you're sick and you need someone to take care of you? What about when you've had a bad day and you just need someone to complain to? What about at night, when it's cold and you just wish someone was beside you? And not just for a night but every night. I don't know. It just sounds nice to me."

Helly thought about Tom and Mandy. She thought about Samantha's parents. She wondered about her own parents and what their marriage had been like. Perhaps if she could find out, she might be able to better anticipate and prepare for her own future.

Master Quon's Karate Dojo, Richfield

This is amazing! Hebruce thought to himself. He'd been working with Helly for two weeks now. All of the karate training he'd received up until this point felt as if he'd been rubbing sticks together, but now he was finally starting to see some smoke. She was adding the missing ingredients to his practice that was elevating him to a new level of performance and focus. It was as if he was channeling his hero and namesake. In silence, the two of them moved around the mat like prowling cats, their movements fluid and stealth-like. Each wore neutral but attentive expressions, their eyes locked in a mutual trance. One would begin to close and the other would adjust either to avoid contact or to defend against it.

When his mom had signed him up four years ago, all he could think about was seeking revenge on the bullies at his school. Going to sleep at night, he would dream about being surrounded by the starting players of their football team as the entire school gathered to witness the imminent and morbid spectacle. Then, as they all pounced simultaneously into a big dogpile to beat him to a pulp, one by one they would fly away through the air as his fists of fury dealt out some schoolyard justice.

Now, he was learning that being prepared to defend yourself would actually reduce both the need and opportunity to go on the offensive.

"Conservation of energy." Helly instructed as she

circled. "A human body does not have the capacity for prolonged combat, especially if poorly conditioned. Enduring the first wave of assault will give you a great advantage in warfare. Cause your opponent to exert themselves, wait until their adrenaline has been exhausted. Avoid using yours at all."

Suddenly, they were locked in a knot of arms, wrists and hands. Hebruce held his own, but he suspected that she was allowing him to. He struggled to gain the mechanical advantage.

"Stay calm. War is work," she quietly reminded.

Hebruce further settled himself and thought more while struggling less. Using an Aikido principle, he applied pressure toward her until he felt her push back. Quickly, he reversed his effort and pulled her toward him. He clutched her arms tightly and rolled backward in an effort to flip her. Then, like all the other times, he felt quick impacts on his forearms as she cartwheeled through the air, making a graceful arc overhead. She twisted and landed lightly, nodding her approval. "Very good. You are improving."

Byerton University Campus

It was after 8:00 PM and the science building was completely empty except for two students.

"I've spent so many late nights here, the faculty decided it was just easier to give me a key," Harmon explained.

Matthew wasn't surprised. *It's not like he's gonna be out on a date.*

They walked to a lockbox mounted near a door labeled "lab" where Harmon removed another key, which allowed them to enter what he referred to as "sacred ground." Then, he reverently removed a tray of test tubes, jars and various pieces of lab equipment. Setting it down on a nearby lab table, his eyes remained focused on the items as he uttered, "There it is. DD-219."

"Is that supposed to mean something to me?"

"Well, the 219 represents how many attempts it took to figure it out."

"What about the DD?"

"Desire Drug. Please don't tell anybody. I know it's lame."

"Whatever." Considering what he had to gain from being included in this science experiment, Matthew's disposition was less than supportive.

Harmon used a pair of large metal tweezers to remove a single pill from a prescription type bottle. He placed it on what looked like a blue napkin and then looked at Matthew expectantly.

"Now, think of something that you'd really rather not do right now."

"OK. I'd rather not be spending this evening in a science lab."

Harmon frowned. "Come on. I'm serious. I want you to see how this works firsthand."

Matthew closed his eyes and finally said. "OK. It would be beneath me to clean the toilets in the bathroom."

"That's perfect!" Then he nodded toward the pill.

"What? You want me to take it?"

"Sure! Medically, it's harmless. It metabolizes completely out of your system in twelve hours. Just think of it as a light switch. What is currently turned off is about to be turned on."

"Turned on? You're not gonna do anything weird are you?"

"Bad analogy. It's not going to hurt you. I've tried it myself multiple times but that initiates an automatic bias to my results."

Reluctantly, Matthew picked up the pill, smelled it and then tossed it in his mouth. A big gulp and it was down. He waited expectantly but nothing seemed to happen.

"I still don't want to clean the toilets. Fail."

Harmon smiled, "You forgot. It needs alcohol to be activated." He picked up a tiny cup that looked like a stainless-steel shot glass and offered it to him.

Once again, he smelled it then threw his head back in the expected manner as he drank the liquid. He set down the cup and looked at Harmon. Harmon watched his specimen the way Dr. Frankenstein watched his monster.

The skepticism and disdain seemed to soften in Matthew's eyes. His presence was more amiable and the corners of his mouth lifted ever so slightly.

Harmon gave the drug a few more moments to take effect. Then he asked, "Hey, Matthew. Whaddaya think about giving the bathroom a quick clean? I noticed earlier that the toilets need some attention." Harmon waved his hand in front of his nose as he made a face of disgust.

Matthew shrugged and said, "We probably should. Everyone appreciates a clean bathroom."

A huge smile crept across Harmon's face. He unconsciously rubbed his hands together the way you see mad scientists do in the movies. *It's working!* he thought with pure glee. He decided to take the experiment one step further. "Tell you what, buddy. I really need to finish up here in the lab. You go take care of the bathrooms and I'll be in to check on you in just a few minutes."

Matthew smiled and pointed playfully toward Harmon. "You're gonna be impressed! Those bowls are gonna be gleaming." He turned and almost skipped as he headed toward his adored latrine duties.

Samantha's Home,
Simmons Lane, Richfield

Helly watched as Samantha stood in front of her dresser mirror, applying lipstick to puckered lips. She, herself, had never used makeup and really didn't understand the point. However, in the defense of makeup users everywhere, not everyone was blessed with her naturally tan skin tone and clear complexion. Maybe it was her lifetime absence of any skin products. Maybe it was her diet. Maybe it was the clean air of the Songshan Mountains.

"I'm finding someone older," Samantha declared resolutely to Helly as well as to her own reflection.

"How much older? Perhaps one of Tom's friends?"

"Ooh, gross! He's, like, 30. That would feel like I'm dating my dad."

Helly blinked as she waited for her friend to clarify.

"I read this article in a magazine that says that girls are naturally four years more mature than boys. If that's true, I need to be looking for someone around twenty-one to twenty-five."

Helly's expression was suddenly questioning. "OK. Thirty is too old but twenty-five is acceptable."

"I'm not saying I'm going to date someone that old. I'm just keeping my options open." Samantha began to quickly dab a brush against one closed eyelid and then the other.

"Tom is two years older than Mandy, so he is two years

less mature than her. I hope this does not cause problems in their marriage. Perhaps Mandy should read the article before they have more children."

Samantha shot Helly an amused look. She loved her pragmatic innocence. "Tom and Mandy are fine. There's lots of healthy relationships where the girl is actually older."

"So, you would consider dating a thirteen-year-old boy?"

"Double gross! If I didn't know you, I would think you were joking."

Helly struggled to grasp these unwritten rules of relationships. Apparently, there was no dating manual and nothing was written in stone. "It seems like you are in a delicate stage of life. It sounds very confusing. I will be glad to explain the bears and the trees to you as it was explained to me."

Samantha was lost. "What are the bears and the trees? Is that some Chinese dating ritual?"

Her friend suddenly looked more uncomfortable than she had ever witnessed. Helly cleared her throat and began. "A young man as well as a young woman began to experience changes as they develop into adults. These changes include seeing the other gender as…"

"Whoa! You're talking about the birds and the bees. My parents already mortified me with that talk when I was twelve. Hard pass."

"As I was saying, one suddenly sees the other gender in a romantic sense instead…"

"Helly! Hard pass means I'm not interested. It means no thank you. It means I'd rather jump out of the window than have this conversation – again!"

Helly looked down at the rebuke.

Samantha smiled and sat down beside her friend. She put her arm around her shoulder, pulled her close and said, "I'm sorry, Helly. I'm not upset with you. That is just a REALLY uncomfortable topic for everybody." She paused. "I can't imagine how that talk must have been for you." Samantha thought for a moment. "So, what was it like growing up without a mom? I can't imagine."

Helly composed her words and spoke. "I have not known another experience. My teachers sacrificed greatly to protect me, provide for me and to prepare me. In many ways, they violated centuries of tradition in order to spare me from an uncertain fate. This conversation helps me to realize how awkward it must have been for them." She paused before continuing. "My interactions with Mandy cause me to feel...uncertain."

"Uncertain, how?"

"There are new feelings that I have not experienced before. I do not know where they originate. They have been most unexpected but not at all unpleasant."

With surprising maturity, Samantha said, "Describe how they make you feel."

"I feel a fondness. I feel as if we are becoming attached as when one sews two pieces of cloth together. Each moment or conversation feels like another stitch. When she hugs me and tells me that she is fond of me, it feels like a knot has been tied and that the attachment is permanent. Sadly, I am not sure that it is."

For the first time, Samantha empathized with her friend. She could not imagine going to another country, moving in with some random family and having a future that is so uncertain. She wrapped her other arm around her friend and pulled her into an awkward hug.

"You are so strong, Helly."

Tequilla Time, Richfield

Matthew and Harmon sat on stools at the Mexican themed bar. The whole place was decorated with clay colored tile, fake palm trees and terracotta décor. The owner was Latino, but most of the staff was a blend of Richfield's statistical demographic. It was getting late, close to midnight, which Matthew described as "prime time." He had done his best to help Harmon look the part. Some new clothes, contacts instead of glasses and a more modern haircut had done wonders, but he still lacked the casual swagger of one acquainted with such places.

"Targets sighted, nine o'clock and approaching fast," Matthew said as he swiveled left on his bar stool. Two women who were at least thirty years old had just walked in and were walking toward the bar. Each was wearing skin tight club dresses, high strappy heels and a face full of cosmetics. Apt adjectives would have been "easy" or "loose." As they sat down, Matthew pounced.

"Evening, ladies. How's it going?" His practiced smile was casual yet dazzling. The women looked at each other but did not relay any warning signs. Conversation ensued and soon they were enjoying drinks and laughing loudly. Matthew was really getting into the moment when Harmon tugged on his sleeve.

Matthew turned around and hissed. "What?!? We've got 'em right where we want 'em!"

"This isn't right. These are not suitable conditions for an

experiment. Our results are already tainted."

"What are you talking about?!? These girls are ready to go! Even with you!"

"We are trying to test the drug on UNWILLING test subjects. You don't need me for this."

Despite the excitement of a potential tryst, Matthew realized Harmon was right. With visible disappointment, he turned back toward their two new friends. "Sorry, ladies. We gotta call it a night. My friend here really needs to study."

The two lounge lizards looked surprised and confused. Harmon oddly tipped an imaginary hat in their direction as they stood to leave. Matthew rolled his eyes and shook his head as they headed toward the exit.

Hebruce Lee's Home,
520 Pinheel Drive, Richfield

The computer screen went black after the command was initiated. It held the rapt attention of three young faces. Letters began to emerge like mist, then became solid words: Who is Helly?

The intro faded into the first scene, which was of Helly staring into the camera at close range as she introduced herself. Her blue eyes were almost hypnotic.

"Hello. My name is Helly."

Then the words returned. "Look's American, right? Sounds foreign. Right again."

Helly reappeared and spoke, "I was probably born in America to American parents but I came to be in a monastery in China. That is where I grew up."

The film continued as Helly described what she knew of her origins. As she spoke, scenes from her life over the last several weeks played across the screen. Hebruce has been filming overtly and also discreetly. Because of this, some of the footage looked a little staged, as if they were trying to manufacture a moment. These included clips of Helly riding her bike around the neighborhood, walking around with Mandy as she pushed Maddie in her stroller and hanging out in Samantha's room.

The other clips, however, really gave insight into her day-to-day life. She initially had not been aware that these moments were being recorded, but this first viewing of Hebruce's edited video would be the test to see if they were acceptable for use.

There was Helly at work, white hat and apron, eyes focused on the counter. The footage was taken from within the crowd with the backs of shoulders and heads occasionally appearing in the edges of the frame. She was proficient, precise, efficient and obviously talented. She and Chun were fastidiously preparing orders with the frequent spinning and tossing of knives. Fish and metal glinted in the lights as they were practically juggled through the air between them. There was no checking for cameras to see if she was being recorded. There was no expectation of attention – only a visible desire to do her job well.

The next clip had been taken at the Masons. Hebruce had coordinated with Tom and Mandy to record their evening meal in secret. The conversation over dinner was so congenial, the smiles sincere and the warmth evident. It was very apparent that she was loved.

The next clip was at the dojo. Apparently, Hebruce had hidden the camera under some clothing, which gave the top of the frame an uneven border. He and Helly were on the mat, moving and sparring. She was giving instruction that, as always, was seasoned with a wisdom beyond her years and a straightforwardness that would not be appreciated by everyone. The clip concluded with her evading one of his attempted attacks with her lightning-fast defenses and a stunning acrobatic maneuver. It was undeniably impressive.

The last scene concluded with Helly expressing her hope that she could somehow reconnect with any possible relatives here in the States. She looked directly at the camera, her blue eyes framed by dark brown hair, and offered a supplication. "If you knew my parents, if their passing had significance to you, I would appreciate the information you possess. If we share common blood, I would like the opportunity to know you." She paused before ending with a slight bow of her head and a simple, "Thank you."

As the video ended, Hebruce looked to Helly and waited for her reaction. Samantha was actually blotting her eyes with her palms.

"You have done well in preparing this. Thank you, Hebruce."

He was unusually surprised (and a little delighted) as she placed a hand behind his shoulder and the other around his ribcage, pulling him into a clumsy hug. Even though they had been wrapped up countless times at the dojo, it had never felt like this. He quickly and eagerly returned the gesture, soaking in every millisecond of it.

After a moment, he regained his composure and said, "Alright, I'll get this posted and see what kind of response we get. No promises but you never know. Every once in a while, something on social media can go viral and spread like wildfire." The next week would be very telling.

Burgerzone, Richfield

Samantha was giddy with excitement. Her voice was almost shrill, her hands danced in the air as she spoke and her face could not contain her smile.

"We're going to a party!" she announced to Helly with something more than jubilation.

Helly sat there expressionless as she absorbed the news. "Are we celebrating the passing of one's life increments?"

"What? No. Not some lame birthday party. This is legit. We...are going...to a frat party!" She had the same enthusiasm as a game show host revealing the grand prize.

"I am not familiar with the frat party."

"OK. Let me explain it to you. Remember a few weeks ago when I said that I needed to be dating older guys? Well, two of them came right up and started talking to me when I was at the mall. One of them noticed me and then nudged his friend. I thought for sure that they were looking at someone behind me but they walked right up!" Her voice rose in pitch as she relived the moment. "I was trying so hard to play it cool, but one of them was sooooo good looking. Seriously, he could be on a magazine cover."

"Was the other desirable in appearance?"

She waved a flat palm in the air. "Ehhh. He wasn't awful. Maybe if the other guy hadn't been there, he would have been alright. They didn't really seem to go together. Maybe good-looking guys also have a 'pretty girl's friend.'"

Helly did not get this reference.

"Anyway, they introduced themselves and asked me my name. Then, they invited me, well, us to a party!"

"So, this is the frat party you speak of? I can only deduce that to frat is similar to fraternizing. Is this not synonymous with the act of partying?"

"I think it's actually short for fraternity. It basically means a house full of guys. Each frat house is identified by some Greek alphabets and the girls have their own groups called sororities."

"Would we not be more accepted at a...soroty?"

Samantha ignored the mispronunciation. "That's not the point, Helly. These are college guys! Everyone at school will freak out when they hear that we were hanging out at a frat house."

Helly's expression reflected concern. "You said that we were invited. I have not been acquainted with these young men. Perhaps I could ask Tom and Mandy to have them over for dinner and thus receive their guidance?"

Samantha rolled her head around her shoulders because an eye roll would not suffice. "Nooooo! We're not even telling Tom and Mandy about the guys. Do you want to end this before it even starts? And we're not telling my parents either. Understand?" Her tone was suddenly sterner that Helly had ever heard.

"I do not understand. The use of secrecy is typically used in attacking one's enemy, a delicate matter or a subversive affair. I assume this is the latter."

"Yeah. The third one sounds good. So, you understand that we can't let my parents or your...guardians know about this. Comprende?"

"Please explain why we are withholding our intended whereabouts from our advisors. This seems, what do you often say, shady."

"Listen, Helly. We are still a little too young to be in this crowd. They probably thought I was like nineteen or twenty. But we can't miss this! It could be the start of a whole new era for us! I can't go back to high school babies when there's real men showing interest in me."

Helly thought several moments before answering. "This does not feel like a worthy pursuit. But I want to be supportive of you and assist you in avoiding the life of an old maid."

It wasn't the affirmation she would have preferred but, by Helly standards, it was acceptable.

The Mason's Home,
Simmons Lane, Richfield

It was Tuesday evening at the Masons and the four of them were seated around the table. Shockingly, fish was tonight's main entrée. Neither Tom nor Mandy could quite put their finger on it, but the mood was off. Helly, although never very expressive, was unusually reticent (if that were possible). Like any person in a circle of trust, they silently wondered if they'd done anything to offend her.

"So, do you have any plans for the weekend?" Tom asked innocently.

Despite her natural discipline, she could not completely conceal her apprehension. Her eyes widened and her voice was slightly tense as she stammered, "Samantha wants to spend time together this Friday. It may require spending the night with her. Would this be acceptable?"

Tom and Mandy exchanged glances before she answered. "In America, we call this a sleepover. It just means that you are spending the night with a friend. You usually stay up late, eat popcorn, watch movies, talk about boys."

Helly was walking a tightrope of honesty and was just one misstep away from a precipitous plummet into falsehood. "We would be spending the evening together. I am not certain it will include the aforementioned activities."

They both saw in Helly the reluctance and avoidance they had exhibited toward their parents when they were teenagers. Mandy spoke again. "Helly, we love and care for you very much. We also realize that we are not your parents. You are a very bright girl with more wisdom than us at times. We know you will make good decisions. However, if you ever find yourself in a situation where you don't feel comfortable, we want you to know that you can reach out to us and we will be there. No judgment. No condemnation. We only want good things for you."

Tom thought, *I couldn't have said it better myself.*

Helly looked down at the table as she contemplated this withholding of information from people who had been so good to her. Even without overt lying, it felt deceptive and wrong. The otherwise delicious meal was not enjoyable to her. Her stomach felt sour.

Master Quon's Karate Dojo, Richfield

Hebruce stopped in his tracks as his hands fell to his side.

"I don't like this, Helly."

Helly stared back, seemingly unaffected by his concern. "Samantha says this is an important opportunity. She is concerned that she will be an old maid unless she is courted by a more mature man."

Hebruce rolled his eyes. "Helly, you are so...naïve. I realize you didn't grow up here, but nothing good happens at a frat party. It's organized hedonism with a stamp of approval from the college."

She didn't understand the context.

He took a more earnest tack. "Listen, Helly. I like you very much as a friend and a person. You are the most unique and interesting girl I have ever known." He let his true feelings slip when he added, "You're irreplaceable."

Helly stared back with no reaction. It made it difficult to know if his words were landing. "Your typical frat guy has one objective and he will use whatever tools he has available to achieve that goal, usually alcohol. After a few drinks, girls will consent to do things they would never otherwise do. I know I sound like a prude right now, but it happens even in high school. Older guys prey on girls like you. And, Samantha..." another eye roll, "she is almost desperate. I've seen girls like her who want so badly to be loved that they'll

247

do almost anything for some guy's attention. Look around you. Do you not see how girls dress? The makeup? The hair? The jewelry? They want attention. They know that skin turns guy's heads so they show it."

Helly had not received so much "guidance" or "preaching" or "nagging" since she'd been here. For some reason, only half of her appreciated it. It was oddly irritating to the other half.

"We should continue our practice," she said with finality.

With a look of defeat and heartbreak, Hebruce reluctantly resumed his defensive stance.

Buckston's Grocery, Richfield

The shift had gone as well as any other. There had been a steady stream of spectators. They received the usual "Oohs" and "Ahhs" and even a round of applause as they completed the evening's last order.

She and Chun took off their aprons, which were amazingly clean considering the type of work they did. They were cleaning their work surface and knives when it spilled out of Helly's mouth.

"I am going to a frat party."

Chun looked up as if someone had poked him in the rear with a pin. His eyes widened at this news, not because it was necessarily shocking, but because she was revealing something personal to him. They had been coworkers, a trainee and her trainer, subordinate and superior. Now, there was suddenly a breach in decorum.

He slowly turned to her and tried to sound natural as he stammered, "Oh yeah? Is this up at Byerton?"

"Yes. It is taking place this Friday night. My friend and I have been invited."

He looked uneasy as he asked, "Aren't you seventeen? You don't have any family here, right?"

"You are correct on both accounts. These are statements of concern. You are the third and fourth person to express this emotion. Would you please explain why?"

He was a little confused as to how he could be the third and fourth person, but he knew communication with Helly always included a little static. He of all people could relate. This was truly an uncomfortable topic for him since he had no kids, no wife, not even a significant other at the present.

"Helly, you are a sweet kid. You have been so different from any other girl who has ever worked here. The girls that usually go to frat parties don't have a good head on their shoulders. They're usually the ones with miniskirts, showing their midriffs and waking up the next morning with a boatload of regrets." Maritime analogies were a normal part of his vernacular.

Helly digested his words. He had no vested interest in her yet he obviously cared. His last words were something she would contemplate until the fateful day arrived.

"In our fishing village, we had a saying about girls who were very free with their standards. 'What you catch depends on the type of bait you use.'"

Byerton University Campus

Harmon looked as if he was entering a sacred shrine. The Sigma Omega Alpha house reeked of masculinity and testosterone. Anyone who was not a lifelong jock or a son of wealthy parents needn't apply. He was neither and therefore had no business there. However, Matthew had brought him and smoothed the way with the other guys. It had been agreed upon that he would be outfitted in his usual attire, which included a tight-fitting polo shirt tucked in at the waist, white sneakers and, of course, his bookish glasses. With a sincere desire to produce an accurate test of DD-219's efficacy, he wanted to retain the same repulsion that had faithfully accompanied him up until this point.

Matthew refused to budge. When it was suggested that he dress down, mess up his hair, maybe wedge some spinach between his teeth, he outright refused. *Not one shred of dedication toward science,* Harmon lamented silently.

Going through the actual written checklist, Matthew was mentally marking off the items one by one. "Keg of beer – check. Wine coolers – check. Vodka – check. Tequila – check. Margarita mix – check. Music – check. Snacks – check."

Harmon had done his part. He had portioned out specific doses of DD-219 in powder form, which could be easily added to any drink. Cleverly, they had been poured into those little wooden umbrellas that would be added to the ladies' drinks. He and Matthew wore colorful Hawaiian leis around their necks to support this ruse. They were expecting the DD-219 to take over at that point and do its magic. Matthew was calculating the street value just at Byerton alone if this worked as Harmon had promised.

Instead of actually cleaning up, the other guys were stuffing clothes and cans into any drawer or closet they could find. Air fresheners were sprayed and cologne was applied liberally. "Do Not Disturb" signs had been distributed to each bedroom upstairs along with candles and stainless-steel wine buckets. It was a classy touch in their young, cunning minds.

Samantha's Home,
Simmons Lane, Richfield

Samantha finished applying what appeared to be the third coat to her face. Honestly, she looked years older and strangely unfamiliar. Helly watched as the ceremonial procedure continued with the addition of large earrings and a necklace. As she looked at Samantha's dress, the words of Chun rang in her ears. It was pink, skintight, short and had a large gap, revealing her lower stomach. Samantha was finally filling out after a very slender adolescence.

Giving herself a final evaluation, she turned to Helly. "OK. You're next."

Helly had, at times, wondered how condemned prisoners felt being led to the gallows. Her own stomach felt unsettled and heavy as Samantha grabbed a makeup brush. Twenty minutes later, Helly opened her eyes to see the finished product. A stranger stared back at her from the mirror. She looked flashy and hollow. She marveled at the transformation even as warning alarms rang in her head.

Hebruce Lee's Home,
520 Pinheel Lane, Richfield

Hebruce sat at his desk. Usually, the stream of comments and likes was more than enough to occupy his thoughts but, tonight, they were troubled. Nausea filled his gut as his mind fabricated multiple worse case scenarios involving Samantha and Helly. He slammed his fist onto the desk in frustration as he complained to the empty room. "How could you be so stupid, Samantha? Why drag Helly into your childish games?"

He felt aggravated, frustrated and impotent to intervene. His evening would pass slowly and tortuously.

The Mason's Home,
Simmons Lane, Richfield

They washed the dishes in silence. Helly's empty chair had cast a somber parlor over the evening. Even Maddie was quiet, which only added to the foreboding mood.

"I don't feel good about this," Mandy declared.

Tom just nodded his agreement.

"Should we have said more?" she asked.

"I don't know. It's a strange arrangement. For weeks, she's seemed like a Godsend and now, it's like dark clouds have rolled in to ruin our picnic." He had always been poetic with his metaphors.

"I'm really worried about her. What would we do if something happened to her? Should we be prepared...just in case?"

Tom was substantially wise for his age, almost equal to his wife. As male minds typically work, he had been stoically analyzing various fixes for hypothetical problems that could arise with Helly. Unfortunately, none of them were proactive. With absolutely no physical course of action for the here and now, he offered to petition a higher authority.

"Would you pray with me?"

They held hands and bowed their heads as he began. "Father, thank You for sending us Helly..."

Byerton University Campus

Music, light and life were pouring out of the open doors of the Sigma Omega Alpha house. It served as a beacon of relief from the tedium of study and stress that occurred during class hours throughout the week. To say it was an open invitation was not entirely true. It was the unspoken duty of the frat brothers to all serve as bouncers for the unwelcome. This included nerds, dorks, goths, uggos, fatties and narcs. They also served as lookouts for adults, staff or any other form of authority.

Samantha and Helly stopped on the sidewalk and gazed up at the bastion of debauchery, a mixture of fear and curiosity pumping through their hearts. Samantha was ready to walk the aisle and say "I do." Helly felt like she was being led into an ambush.

They watched other girls entering and tried to mimic their behavior. They swaggered in high heels, sometimes arm in arm. They shouted to those inside and stuck their fists into the air with loud *woohoo*s. Properly motivated, Samantha followed suit and stuck her arm through Helly's. She was relieved when Matthew and Harmon appeared just inside the door. Helly unconsciously evaluated both men, seeing no threat in the smaller one but detecting a sinister darkness in the taller one. It was an intrinsic side effect of her training. Perhaps it was body language, pheromones or just the eyes, but she always knew. However, Matthew countered with a distractingly warm smile and a natural charm that could make a librarian swoon.

Their coats were taken as they entered, and then they were offered a drink. Without hesitation, Samantha took the red solo cup with the tiny umbrella and took a gulp. She had already settled her scruples. Helly took the cup and instinctively sniffed it. Matthew and Harmon were watching closely. "What is this?" she asked flatly.

"Just some punch. We're famous for it. We also have margaritas and beer if that's your thing."

Samantha shuttered with embarrassment as Helly asked, "Do you have anything without alcohol?"

Matthew, smooth as a serpent, said, "Sure! Let me run to the kitchen." He returned shortly with an actual glass. It was red with crushed ice, some fruit and (of course) one of those little umbrellas. "It's a virgin Hurricane. No alcohol. Not everyone on campus likes to drink," he added.

She reluctantly took the glass and took a tentative sip. It was fruity and tasty and so cold. As her defenses began to abate, she took another larger sip. She could have sworn that Matthew winked at his smaller friend.

Hebruce Lee's Home,
520 Pinheel Drive, Richfield

Hebruce was now short circuiting. Try as he may, he could not distract himself with any of his usual entertainment. The thought of something irrevocable happening to Helly consumed the entirety of his thoughts. He cursed himself for only being a seventeen-year-old senior. He cursed himself for not having a car, or a driver's license for that matter. He cursed himself for being a thin Asian with mediocre martial arts skills at best. The words of Master Quon came to mind. "By failing to prepare, you are preparing to fail." *Aggghhhh!!! This is infuriating!* He wanted to punch something. He wouldn't mind if someone punched him. He felt as if he deserved it for being less than what he needed to be right now.

Main Street, Richfield

Chun's Hyundai sedan cruised north toward The Feeding Trough. He looked like a huge guerilla stuffed inside of the small import. However, it had been in his price range and he'd always viewed anything from South Korea in a positive light.

Like most Friday nights, he would grab his take-out order, pick up a couple of movies at the rental box and spend the evening alone on his couch. Later that evening, with a full stomach and numb mind, he would fall asleep, sometimes in his bed, sometimes right there on the sofa. It was an existence and not much more.

Byerton University Campus

Harmon was elated with the results. Samantha was sitting in his lap with her arms around his neck. With complete abandon, she kissed him on the lips. Warmth spread over him as her scent and softness inundated his senses. It was an entirely new sensation to him. Like a man being pulled in the current towards the lip of a waterfall, he was going with the flow.

Matthew, on the other hand, had set his sights on a more formidable adversary. Ditzy college girls weren't really a challenge for him anymore. His routine was the product of a time-honored formula. Countless players before him had passed down the skills of seduction through their performances on the big screen. He'd also learned from the examples set by big brothers and older classmen.

As he set his sights on Helly, he was unable to get a clear shot. She was an enigma. Besides her staccato robotic language, her mannerisms were cool and reserved. She didn't fall for the usual traps and snares that he casually set for all of his previous trophies. He decided that he would have to lay the dreaded groundwork that was required for more reluctant prey. He would have to actually talk.

Helly, on the other hand, did not perceive the letting down of her guard. The drink had been tasty so she'd had another. *Why not? Humans must drink to survive. And being here? There was no perceivable danger. Everyone was smiling. Smiling is a natural human practice to indicate that you mean no harm.* She had even lost her suspicion of Matthew. She admitted that he was attractive by American standards (or even her own).

He gestured toward the couch and wanted to know more about her. "So, Helly. Tell me your story. Did you grow up around here?"

He's so nice. He's interested in me. He makes me feel special, important to him. With no governor in place, she lets the words flow and allowed him access to her heart.

Matthew recognized this and silently congratulated himself. *Works like a charm.*

The Mason's Home,
Simmons Lane, Richfield

It was bedtime. Mandy stood by the window and pulled the blinds down to check the street once more. She knew it was pointless.

"I know she's not at Samantha's."

"I don't so think so, either," Tom said from the bed.

"Should we call Samantha's parents?"

"I dunno. I wasn't expecting to deal with situations like this for another fifteen years or so. What if we called and everything is fine? Would she trust us in the future? And what if Helly wanted to go off the deep end? Do we have any right to stop her?"

Mandy had been wrestling with identical thoughts the entire evening. "I'm not sure I want Maddie to become a teenager if this is what it's like."

Tom looked vacantly toward the foot of the bed. "Me either."

Byerton University Campus

Matthew and Harmon had simultaneously excused themselves to the kitchen under the guise of getting more drinks. They quickly conferred their observations. Harmon started.

"It's working! She's really into me. You agree that she's way out of my league, right?"

Matthew loathed his business partner but agreed. "Yes. She's way out of your league." He also wondered if Harmon realized that she was underage. Sure, it happened all the time, but there were potential consequences lingering out there. It was kind of like going outside in a lightning storm. You could get struck but probably not. He could have doubted the effects of DD-219 and attributed her willingness to the alcohol. However, he knew from experience that what was taking place was more than inebriation.

"Yeah, man. Way to go! When I first saw her friend, she was as cold as ice. But have you seen her now? She is ready to go." Hormones and a healthy dose of beer had also erased his fear of legal reprisal.

In a rare moment of comradery, he slapped Harmon on the shoulder, smiled and said "OK. Time to seal the deal."

John Cleveland

Hebruce Lee's Home,
520 Pinheel Drive, Richfield

There comes a time in a man's life when he has to decide. *Am I going to just sit here and do nothing – or am I going take action?* Hebruce had been wrestling with this dilemma all night. Temptations of fear had been paralyzing him with indecision.

What if I find her and she doesn't want to be rescued?

What if I embarrass her and she never talks to me again?

What if someone wants to fight and I wuss out?

He had reached a tipping point. He either needed to go to sleep and try to put her out of his mind, or he could use whatever he had and step out into the unknown. He looked once more upon the wall where a framed poster of Bruce Lee offered his trustworthy advice. It showed his hero standing shirtless with clinched fists, rippled muscles and a look of determination. Printed above the photo was the phrase, "Fear is for others."

He popped out of bed, grabbed his hachimaki headband and headed toward the door.

Byerton University Campus

Matthew was lighting the candles and adjusting the bottle of champagne, which was now chilling in the bucket of ice. Although the loud thumping party music could still be heard through the closed door, he had what he thought was romantic, mood setting music playing through his smartphone on the nightstand.

Helly felt completely agreeable to being here. He was being so nice and friendly and gentle. *Maybe Samantha had been right all along. Could I imagine being married to Matthew? It was not uncommon for teenagers to be married. Surely, that's where all of this was heading. This would be a good thing.*

In the room next door, Harmon was fumbling with straps and buttons. His lack of experience was really showing, but Samantha couldn't care less. She would have given him her debit card and pin number if he'd asked for it. *Tonight is a dream. Harmon is the man of my dreams. So...he's so...he's just like I always...* Her thoughts did not calculate. This man had none of the attributes she had wanted in a guy yet she saw absolutely no reason to refuse him. Under other circumstances, even she would have registered concerns about health risks, unplanned pregnancies and possibly the emotional consequences of such a fling. But not tonight. She was more in the moment than she had ever been in her life. Unusually so.

-

Had security been patrolling the main entrance to the campus, they would have observed a very determined young man wearing a black headband, pedaling a blinged-out bike like Lance Armstrong. His jaw was clinched as he blew out breaths in quick puffs through pursed lips. The sound of club music and young people laughing led the way.

A few people noticed the newcomer as he skidded into the yard, laid down the bike and marched toward the front door. His eyes were set and his hands were balled into fists. A few of the bigger guys laughed and pointed, their comments less than complimentary.

Hebruce was about to make entry into the house when two large guys stepped into his path. Their combined weight equaled over three of him. It was too late to back down now.

"I'm here for Helly," he spat with as much rancor as he could muster. The two jocks, fueled by conceit and bravado, looked at each other and laughed. Hebruce stuck out his slender arms and tried to push between them. Instantly, he found his arms locked in vises as his feet left the floor. He was turned around in midair and displayed like a criminal on a cross. Then, without the slightest trace of dignity, he was tossed off the porch and over the yard like a bag of unwanted garbage. As he clumsily landed in the grass, the laughter of several nearby girls stung worse than his injuries. *This would not have happened to Bruce.*

Upstairs, things were getting intense and it was

primarily due to DD-219. Equal to Matthew's desire was his forethought about making money. Even as he unbuttoned his shirt, he was formulating distribution networks and laundering schemes. Mentally, he was already selecting the leather interior for the Porsche 911 that he would soon be driving. He thought he heard a brief commotion downstairs, but that was not uncommon at these parties. Anyways, he'd be back down in a few minutes to see if he'd missed any action.

Hebruce's mind was working overtime. The milliseconds drug by as despair, desperation and adrenaline guided his thoughts. He wanted to explode and become the Incredible Hulk but, realistically, he would only find himself flying through the air again like Peter Pan.

Helly came to his mind. He thought about their many sessions in the dojo. He thought about how infuriating her proverbs about warfare had initially been. He also realized that she would have successfully defeated the two ogres at the door and stormed the castle. Maybe now was good time to test the Helly method.

Very much like his hero, he slowly stood and dusted himself off. He even wiped his open mouth with the back of his hand. Laughing girls suddenly became silent as they watched this would-be warrior walk back up the steps and stand before the gloating giants.

"I need to find my friend. She is inside and I am going in there."

One of the brutes looked at his friend. "Whaddaya think? Atomic wedgie or toilet bowl swirly?"

Before his friend could answer, his face contorted in pain as the air hissed from his lungs. His eyes were wide as he sank down onto the wooden slats. Hebruce had delivered a swift kick to the front portion of his ankle, right where it met the shin. He followed up with a quick punch to his sternum, rotating his hips to generate maximum momentum. Someone his own size could have been serious injured, but Hebruce reasoned that he was a big guy and had probably done worse to others.

It took a moment for the other still functional beast to realize he was now alone. He turned to confront and pummel this little intruder when he was suddenly face to face with the shorter foe. Hebruce leaped upward, one knee targeting the crotch of his rival. As he reached the apex of his ascent, he locked his hands around the other man's neck. As his foe doubled over in pain, Hebruce pulled the large head down in a quick motion. As soon as his feet touched the deck, he brought his other knee up into the guard's face. He felt the cracking of the man's bone and cartilage translating through his own skeletal structure. He, like his friend, went down in a heap.

Girls and guys alike watched with open mouths as Hebruce stepped over their fallen bodies and then stopped to look around.

Matthew and Harmon were moments away from achieving tonight's conquests. It was nothing more to either of them. They cared nothing for these girls and even less about any harm they may be doing. Sadly, they were also denying themselves the opportunity for true intimacy in the future. There would be little desire to show respect. There would be no exclusivity. Emotional bonds would be formed only to be mercilessly severed in the morning light.

BOOM!!! The door to Matthew's room burst open with the blinding glare from the hallway lights. He shielded his eyes to see the silhouette of a smaller male figure standing in the doorway. The untimely interruption became rage in his veins. He leapt from the bed, mostly undressed by now and faced his challenger. "You broke into the wrong room tonight, Small Fry."

Normally, his words would have been hurtful. But not tonight. Not in this frame of mind. Hebruce stood his ground and examined his opponent. Matthew was a good six inches taller. He outweighed him by at least fifty pounds and probably had more fighting experience. Or did he? Hebruce had been putting in the work. Years of lessons recently coupled with Helly's instruction had changed him. Maybe he wasn't completely harmless.

He looked past Matthew and saw Helly sitting in the bed, sheets pulled up to her bare shoulders. Her face was almost unrecognizable. It wasn't just the colored powder and lip gloss, but the at ease expression. She looked very relaxed and content and registered no surprise that he was now here. Something was not right.

The action had stopped next door as well. Harmon heard the concussion and cracking of wood. He was already on edge and it didn't take much to derail him. He decided to investigate.

-

Matthew stood, hating this intruder. "Who are you?" he demanded with a few added expletives.

"I'm here for Helly. She shouldn't be here."

Matthew turned to look at his bedmate and offered smugly. "She looks pretty willing to me. Do you think she'd rather be with a little shrimp like you?"

"I know Helly and something is not right. You have done something to her."

Matthew's face betrayed his sudden fear of discovery. Doubts began to seep in like leaks in a dam. He couldn't immediately come up with a comeback.

"I knew it! You've drugged her or something. And after I get through beating you, I'm calling the police."

Matthew grinned knowing that Step #2 couldn't happen unless Step #1 did. He grinned at the certainty of his forthcoming victory. He lunged into the air and was preparing to deliver a vicious downward blow into Hebruce's face. It would carry the weight of his entire body plus the force of his muscles. However, he struck only thin air and tumbled onto the floor as nothing resisted his momentum.

He turned around and saw Hebruce now somehow standing just inside of the room. He rose and charged again, going for a football style tackle. Just before impact, he felt hands helping him along and increasing his speed as his face struck a large, wooden corner post of the bed. The collision made his vision blur as his eyes began to water.

Now blind with fury, he turned to find Hebruce standing near the nightstand. *Now, he's cornered. Time to finish this,* Matthew seethed to himself. Instead of a frontal assault, he wrapped up Hebruce in a huge bear hug and lifted him off the ground, his legs struggling for purchase and finding none. Matthew then squeezed with all of his might, hoping to crack some ribs or suffocate the little twirp.

Hebruce had yet to be in this position in his training. He felt the vise-like pressure increasing and realized that he only had seconds to act, his consciousness beginning to ebb as the pressure from Matthew's grip increased. He looked down at Helly, who seemed oddly detached and merely observant. Thankfully, the thought that she had been taken advantage of provided the strength he needed at this moment. Love is truly stronger than hate.

Hebruce wriggled his right arm up just enough to regain some flexibility in his elbow. He slipped it around Matthew's head and allowed his own body weight to slip over toward the bigger man's back. As Matthew's balance began to teeter backward, Hebruce applied more pressure and let all of his one hundred and thirty pounds assist him. He tightened the noose and felt Matthew's grip around him start to weaken.

Matthew was starting to see stars and was at a loss. *How is this happening?* It was the last conscious thought he would have for several moments. In seconds, both bodies fell to the ground like twin towers.

Hebruce extricated himself and quickly turned to Helly. The situation demanded that he be very straightforward.

"Helly, they have put something in your drink. They've drugged you. You need to come with me right now!" He was preparing to take her out by force, if necessary. She would understand later after the drug wore off. Instead, her response was pleasingly agreeable.

"Sure! Why not?" She smiled and hopped out of bed as

she began putting on her jeans and shirt. He instinctively turned around even though his eyes would have enjoyed the sight.

He was leading her out of the room, guiding her as if she was physically disabled. He didn't know what else to do. As he entered the hallway at the top of the stairs, he met an unknown player in tonight's contest. A much less intimidating guy, just slightly older than himself and roughly his equivalent physically, was standing just outside of the nearest room. He was wearing only tighty-whitey underwear and holding something pink in his right hand.

Suddenly, Samantha was peeking from the open door beside him, a bedsheet wrapped around her like a towel. She recognized Hebruce with innocent delight. "Hi, Hebruce! I didn't know you were coming to the party. There are drinks in the kitchen."

Something is definitely off with these two, he thought.

After the three confrontations he had just survived, Hebruce felt a great sense of relief seeing that his next nemesis was somehow pale, pudgy and skinny all at once. If great physiques were built in the gym, this one was built in the lab. As confidence began to fill up his ego, the other man's hand raised and Hebruce recognized the object as pepper spray. He held up his hands, shut his eyes and turned his head, but he felt the liquid drizzling across his forehead and nose.

Hebruce braced for instant, mind-numbing agony but nothing really happened. He even ventured to open his eyes, which would prove to be a mistake. He tasted and smelled a slight chemical odor and maybe something akin to spices. Then, it got warm.

Like a volcano, the heat of lava began to pour over his features. It hit his eyes first and then snuck into his respiratory system. A large whiff was inhaled as panic began to interrupt this focus. The searing heat began to increase exponentially so that he'd thought he'd reached the limit of human pain tolerance. Then, it increased even more. He blinked rapidly, but it felt like someone had heated up grains of sand in a skillet and then inserted them under his eyelids. Instinctively, he shot his hands out, crouched and began to feel about like a blind man. For all intents and purposes, he now was.

Helly and Samantha only compounded his problems. Both were in various states of undress and neither saw any reason to be alarmed. He heard Samantha speaking calmy to Helly with no regard for the obvious fact that he was engulfed in invisible flames. "Hi, Helly. Did you know Hebruce was coming? So whaddaya think about Matthew?"

Helly responded in an unusually bright tone. "He's nice. I really hope he's OK."

As their discussion continued, Hebruce felt a very weak punch ricochet off of his cheek. It didn't land and obviously had been poorly thrown. He felt another wave of panic, realizing that he would now have to defend himself without the benefit of vision. Any hope that his friends would snap out of their haze and come to his rescue was squashed when he heard Samantha express her sudden desire for more Doritos. Helly agreed that it was a great idea.

Another impact with greater accuracy stung the top of his head. It felt like an open-handed slap. He blinked wildly and rubbed his face, but it only seemed to smear the liquid fire. The pain intensified several more degrees. His mind was telling him that the heat would rise until he literally burst into flames. It felt like permanent damage was being done to his eyes. He would have hyperventilated, but his lungs adamantly refused to inhale any more of the inflammatory fumes.

It was the third time tonight that every fiber of his being encouraged him to give up.

Time passes slowly when you're under duress. Now in overdrive, his mind was taking in and processing every detail of his pain and panic. His senses were heightened and his emotions were off the chart. His adrenal glands were pumping out adrenaline and drawing from reserves that were nearly depleted.

It's interesting, because there are things about the human psyche that cannot be fully explained. Although his fight-or-flight mechanism was fully endorsing the second option, there was an ember of selflessness that still burned somewhere deep within this moment of darkness. As he recognized this almost invisible light, he remembered his reason for coming. He remembered his two friends. He remembered the deplorable reasons why they had been lured to this loathsome place.

Harmon was surprised when Hebruce suddenly quit gasping and began to blink as he attempted to survey his surroundings. He stood more erect and held his hands up in an intentionally defensive position. Unbeknownst to him, Hebruce was mentally revisiting a moment with Helly that had occurred in the dojo. She had been blabbering on about energy and perceiving one's life force. She compared the ability with knowing when someone behind you is staring at you or turning to see who just walked into a room when you didn't hear them. "We know when others are close by," she'd explained. It had seemed like bunk at the time, but tonight, she was proving her tendency of being right most of the time.

Hebruce was now scanning the area for his target even without vision. Harmon had been feeling victorious but was now feeling a rising sense of dread. His anxiety began to rise as the hunter realized that he had become the hunted. Harmon tried to bolt past Hebruce and shoot down the stairs. As he flailed through the gap, a hand shot out and grabbed his hair. His head flung backward as his momentum was stopped. He found himself bent over backward with the pressure on his scalp solely supporting him. His exposed throat was completely open to a potentially lethal blow. Sufficient anger existed for Hebruce to deliver what many would consider well deserved justice. As Harmon let out a pitiful wail, begging for mercy, Hebruce wiped his hand across his own face and then rubbed it generously over the eyes and nose of Harmon. Seconds later, he began to beg and cry for help.

"Ahh! AHHH! AHHHHH!!! It shouldn't be burning this bad! Help! HELP!!!"

Time was ticking. Others would come. Hebruce needed to move and get the girls out of here right now.

"Samantha! Helly! Please come to me. We need to leave!"

He heard footsteps as they both drew near. He fumbled until he held both of their hands and began to stumble down the steps. As they reached the bottom, an unfortunate student just happened to be in their way, only curious and definitely not aggressive.

"Hey! Are you guys OK?" he asked.

A flat palm shot out blindly from Hebruce, which struck the bystander directly in the ear.

"You jerk! What's the matter with you!" he complained as he put his hand up to the side of his head. His words faded as the trio moved down the steps and toward the road.

.

Monroe Boulevard, Richfield

Chun was just a few blocks from home. His secret musical passion was playing over the speakers.

Don't tell my heart, my achy-breaky heart, I just don't think he'd understand...

He provided an interesting accompaniment with an Asian flair as he drummed along to the country classic on his steering wheel.

From out of nowhere, bodies appeared directly ahead in the street. With eyes as wide as saucers, he stood on the brakes and stopped just feet away from the three pedestrians. In his headlights, he saw a teenage boy. Even though his eyes were swollen shut and his face was flushed, it was still obvious that he too was Asian. Chun noted with curiosity that the young man wore a black martial arts headband. The two girls holding onto him were barely dressed. One still needed to button several buttons on her blouse and the other was wearing a bedsheet. He was about to angrily dismiss them as drunk college kids until he recognized one of the three.

"Helly?"

It was at this same time that Matthew had awakened and assembled the troops. Harmon was out of commission (and not a viable asset anyway). But the two ogres and half a dozen other footballs players were ready to defend their fortress. The agitated mob of men moved toward the street and was closing in on the three people illuminated by the lights of a stopped car less than two feet away.

Chun thought back to his conversation with Helly and quickly connected the dots. She wore a peculiar expression that did not reflect who he knew her to be. Something was not right. The Asian kid and the half-naked girl only confirmed his suspicions. He looked left, observing a group of fired up young men approaching and realized that Helly was potentially in trouble.

With his bullish build and brute strength, he felt completely comfortable with confrontation. A bulldozer does not fear flowers. Matthew and his crew drew near with jaws set and fists clenched. Perhaps if they'd been sober, common sense would have suggested that they were not invincible.

"Keep moving! Mind your own business," Matthew defiantly yelled.

The door to the little Hyundai opened and the suspension raised about two inches as the driver exited. His imposing figure was only exaggerated by his cavalier confidence and expressionless face. Matthew gave the two ogres a slight push forward. In their sudden reverse and retreat, he was pushed backward where he stumbled over the curb before landing on his rear end. One by one, his comrades abandoned him until he was sitting alone on the sidewalk.

Much like Hebruce, a protective ignition had taken

place deep within Chun. He would only admit it recently, but Helly held a special place in his heart. Her life added to his and he would not let her be threatened. He stood over Matthew and glared down at him like a lion drooling over a frightened hare. Instead of a beatdown, the giant man simply took out his cell phone and snapped a photo. It would eventually cause more damage than any pummeling.

Mercy Medical Center, Richfield

The late-night phone call to the Masons had almost been a relief. At least now, the unknowing was over. In their fogginess, shoes were momentarily put on the wrong feet and tags were sticking out of shirts put on inside out. A confused and understandably fussy Maddie was quickly buckled into her car seat seconds before the minivan's tires barked on the pavement as it accelerated toward the hospital.

Chun had calmly loaded the three teens into his small car and driven them to the emergency room. Local police arrived there shortly after. The attending medical staff was a little perplexed at how agreeable the two young ladies were.

"You need to change clothes into this gown."

"Looks nice. Thanks!"

"We need to start an IV. This is going to sting."

"No problem! Sounds great."

Testing the limits of their agreeability, a doctor teasingly suggested, "We are going to recommend to your parents that you be grounded until you're twenty-one and that you voluntarily do community service."

Samantha nodded earnestly and approvingly. "That is an excellent idea. You're the doc, doc."

He exchanged a concerned look with the nurse.

-

Tom almost fought his way past the receptionist in the waiting room as he caught the attention of the security guards. With daily experience of dealing with emotionally charged people, they were able to temper Tom's charge and remind him of how he could be most helpful to whomever he was here to see.

Minutes later, his face hovered over Helly, who was lying in a hospital bed, the steady beeping of the monitors ensuring him that she was very much alive. The tension instantly broke, as did his stoic veneer. He carefully slid his arms around her neck to hug her as tears filled his eyes.

"Thank you, God," he spoke quietly.

He released her and quickly inspected her visually. *No black eyes. No visible cuts or bruises. No visible blood. Maybe somebody won't have to die tonight.*

He was not a confrontational or violent man. Quite the opposite, actually. However, the events of tonight had triggered a capacity for violence that was hidden in the heart of every man who truly loves someone. He took a full breath and blew it out slowly as his frazzled nerves began to relax.

He floundered for the right words. "Helly, we...were so scared. We..." It was more than a little puzzling when she smiled and spoke in a brighter tone than he'd ever heard from her.

"Hi, Tom! How's it going? It sounds like the doctor is going to recommend grounding. This sounds promising."

His bewildered expression was noticed by the doctor, who tried to offer some clarity.

"We believe she and her friend have been exposed to an engineered controlled substance. The lab is running a complete analysis on their blood."

Tom maintained eye contact with the doctor to indicate his attention as he continued.

"According to the man who brought them in, they had been at a frat party up at Byerton. This isn't the first time we've treated someone who became the guinea pig of some chemistry-student-turned-mad-scientist."

The fiery red speck in Tom's heart flared again as he processed the news. *There will be a time and a place for that. For now, let's focus on Helly.*

"Are you the parent or legal guardian of this young lady?" the doctor asked.

Tom's wide eyes indicated that he was searching for the right answer to this question. "I...don't know. She's been living in our garage for the last three months." He looked down sadly as he added, "She doesn't have anyone else."

Thankfully, the critical nature of the emergency room allowed for more flexibility than the typical rigidity of healthcare bureaucracy. He was allowed to stay as he began to give information to the nurse who was filling out "paperwork" on an electronic medical chart.

The arrival of Samatha's parents was even more dramatic as they came barreling into the small room adjacent to Helly's. Loud, rapid-fire questions were directed at their daughter, the doctor and anybody else unfortunate enough to be within eyesight. Thankfully, the staff understood that this was an unavoidable yet expected reaction of loving parents.

For the next three hours, the girls were mostly observed as the intravenous saline continued to dilute whatever mysterious substance had been introduced into their systems. Chun was hugged by the moms and thanked warmly as the events of the evening were revealed in greater detail. Information was given to the uniformed police officers and witness statements were completed. A photo was forwarded from Chun to the phone of the investigating officer.

Poor Hebruce bore his war wounds with dignity. The worst of the pepper spray's effects went away on their own by the time they arrived at the hospital. His eyes and face were still horribly red, but his vision was quickly returning back to normal.

A nurse unofficially examined him, but it was the police officers who gave the best advice. "We've had that crap sprayed on us a few times. Go outside, find a hose pipe and just let it run. Don't rub your eyes or use any soap. It'll feel better."

Chun led him outside and held the nozzle as Hebruce leaned over the makeshift curative fountain. Perhaps the burly man wasn't the brutish beast everyone had assumed.

Byerton University Campus

If Matthew thought his good looks, charm or daddy's money was going to get him out of this one, he was sorely mistaken. Perhaps his greatest mistake was failing to prep his accomplice for just such an occasion. Harmon squealed like a pig as soon as his rights were read. Motivated by fear of prison, he confided in the investigating officer like a guidance counselor. The tape recorder and notepad captured his flowing testimony as he described everything from the almost romantic junction with a minor all the way back to his late-night research in the lab. He even offered samples to the officer, who smartly packaged and labeled them as evidence. Although the repercussions of tonight would affect the next several years of his life, ultimately they would either steer him away from future transgressions or diminish his respect for the rights of others. Only time would tell.

Matthew, on the other hand, would have made his father proud in some sick, strange way. He clammed up and set his face like flint. He wouldn't even give his name as his rights were read and the questioning began. He had been too spoiled in his twenty-one years of life and was way too obstinate to garner any grace with the officers. As his attitude continued to reject any leniency, handcuffs were extracted from a duty belt of an officer, who directed him to turn around and place his hands behind his back. More serious charges would follow later this week as warrants were processed, but Public Intoxication would be a good reason for him to spend the night behind bars tonight. Plus, it set an excellent foundation of evidence for his pending prosecution.

John Cleveland

The Mason's Home,
Simmons Lane, Richfield

There were no morning exercises or meditative practices today. Helly sat in bed as she sternly stared at the shape of her feet underneath the sheets. A little after 9:00 AM, there was a gentle knock on the door to the garage apartment. A moment later, the door cracked open as Mandy shyly entered, a wooden tray held in the crook of her arm. It held a glass of orange juice, a plate of eggs and toast and even a small vase with a single sunflower leaning leisurely against its rim.

Mandy walked over, set down the tray on the nightstand and softly sat down beside her friend. Helly continued to stare without acknowledging her. Time passed with neither saying a word.

Eventually, Mandy tenderly placed her hand on top of Helly's and lightly rubbed the skin between her knuckles and wrist. Touch can often say what words fail to.

Finally, Helly spoke. The old her had returned. "I am stupid. I do not deserve your breakfast. I do not deserve to be your houseguest." Her voice was flat and terse. Any casualness or ease of communication developed over the last several weeks had vanished.

Mandy continued to rub her thumb over the back of Helly's hand. She looked down as if admiring the sheets, her face neutral.

286

Finally, Helly turned to look at Mandy, her face reflecting an expectation or even a desire for a confrontation. "I will package my belongings and depart," she said resolutely.

Mandy lifted her eyes to meet hers and said, "We wish you wouldn't."

Time passed.

Helly's shoulders convulsed once, then again. A strange sound began to emanate from her throat as tears began to roll down her cheeks. Mandy pulled her close and rubbed Helly's back. Something unlocked and was instantly released. All of the tears and motherly consolation that she had been denied for a lifetime poured over the top of the dam. Within seconds it eroded, leaving a wall of pent-up emotion pouring through the valley of her soul.

The eggs and toast became cool as this continued for quite some time. No worries. This was more nourishing and healthful than any meal. Mandy cried with and for her friend as she thought of how many difficult emotional challenges Helly had suppressed over the last fourteen years. Even though Mandy had grown up in an affluent American home with two loving parents, her own teenage years had been full of dramatic moments and emotional roller coasters. At this moment, she mentally committed herself to Helly to be as supportive and helpful as humanly possible. She would invest in the life of this young lady and give to her as much love and support as she would accept.

The next two hours consisted of more talking, crying and laughing than a week of daytime talk shows. Mandy shared stories from her past and, most importantly, she listened. Anyone eavesdropping would have come to the conclusion that Helly was the most amazing girl to ever set foot on American soil and that all men were pigs. Both were absurd exaggerations, but the sentiments were soothing in this setting.

Hebruce Lee's Home,
520 Pinheel Drive, Richfield

Samantha, although grounded, had received permission to visit Hebruce at his home. She had brought a basket full of sports drinks, power bars and a <u>Tiger Claw</u> magazine, which apparently covered all things martial arts. It may have been an odd gift, but it was heartfelt (and within her budget).

Hebruce surprisingly had very few war wounds from his night in the octagon. *He seems...different. More grown up,* she thought. His demeanor did not reflect his usual juvenile swagger and feigned machismo. In their place was an elevated sense of maturity and confidence.

"Thanks, Samantha. I like it," he offered as he took the basket.

She hugged him warmly, looked him in the eyes and said, "Thank you."

He shrugged and continued to display his melancholy as they sat down on the edge of his bed, the door to his room open.

"How are you doing?" she asked. "Are you injured?"

He shrugged. "Not really. My eyes were OK after about an hour of rinsing them with the hose. I just feel strange."

Slightly stunned by the events of the last few days, Samantha was fortunately willing to just listen. He continued.

"It just feels like life is getting more serious. I mean, like, the police showed up. You guys were in the hospital. Those guys were technically adults." He paused. "It just doesn't feel like we're kids anymore. It feels like we've been sucked into a new world that suddenly has real consequences."

Samantha looked down as he said this. He considered how she must be feeling. After all, she'd single-handedly gotten herself and her best friend into a very dangerous situation. He saw a tear form and roll down her cheek.

"Hey, it's OK. You're OK. I'm OK. Helly is OK – I think." He wasn't really sure how to comfort her in an appropriate way, but he felt like a hand on her back would be enough.

"I feel so stupid!" she hissed through gritted teeth. She wrapped her arms across her chest and began to rock back and forth.

He felt like there was more coming, so he waited.

"I don't feel like I will ever be able to make a good decision. It's the first time that my parents have ever grounded me and I wish they had done something worse. I feel like they should send me away to a military school or handcuff me to a nun or..." Other forms of penance eluded her. "I can't believe I did that to Helly." In her defense, it was a sign of maturity that her concern was not focused on herself but her friend. "She has to be so confused. She probably never wants to see me again."

He thought for a moment before sharing his next thoughts. "I didn't realize how much I cared about her until that night." His eyes widened as he made eye contact with Samantha. Quickly he began to backpedal as he tried to modify his confession. "And you! I care about both of you. It's just that we, you know, practice karate and stuff together."

"I get it. You don't have to pretend. I can see it."

"See what?"

"How you feel about her."

Buckston's Grocery, Richfield

Charlie, the manager, was as disappointed as the dissipating crowd at the seafood counter. By himself, Chun wasn't very entertaining. With his typically rueful countenance, he was scornfully chopping off fish heads as he ruminated over the young men who had tried to take advantage of his friend. Mandy had called and explained that Helly needed a few days off and wasn't sure when (or if) she'd be back to work. A percentage of Charlie's heart cared about the well-being of his employee, but the majority of his mind only saw plummeting profits. *Where am I going to find another knife wielding teenage girl that Chun would tolerate?* He was actually biting his fingernails as he considered contacting an international adoption agency.

The Mason's Home,
Simmons Lane, Richfield

The next day, Samantha worked up the courage to knock. All that morning, she had been peeking through her blinds, hoping to catch a glimpse of Helly. She had seen Mandy make a trip out to the garage, later to return with an empty tray, so she felt pretty confident she was in there. She thought about making another gift basket but it just didn't feel anywhere close to sufficient.

After a moment, the door cracked open. Helly looked smaller, or maybe more fragile than she remembered. Something in her stature was off and it filled Samantha's stomach with dread. Fearing that she had somehow permanently hurt her friend, she crumpled emotionally. Tears suddenly burst from a face that was twisted with grief. She moved forward and extended her arms, hoping to be received.

Helly honestly did not know how to respond. She had thought endlessly about what had happened and did not feel anger toward Samantha. She felt angry at herself for falling prey to wretched and worthless men. She felt like she had surrendered to a situation that she was not comfortable with and it had rendered her useless in protecting Samantha. If only human thoughts were visible.

Helly was like a limp ragdoll as Samantha draped her arms over her shoulders and wept. She had been rattled by the last few days, but the warmth of friendship that had been developing over the last several weeks was quickly rekindled. She eventually returned her friend's embrace and enjoyed the comforting relief of their connection.

After emotions subsided, they both tried to speak at once.

"I'm so sorry/I am sorry."

"It's all my fault/I am the one to blame."

"Please forgive me/Please forgive me."

They both let out a relieving laugh as the last phrase was spoken in unison.

Samantha blurted out the next volley, determined to unload her guilty conscience. "Helly, I would never have gotten you into that mess if I had known. It's just – those guys. I thought they really liked me – and Cody had been such a..." It was really just babbling but it needed to come out.

After a few moments, Helly formed her words and spoke. "We were taught an expression in the monastery. When it hurts, observe. Life is trying to teach you something. We can be grateful that our wounds are only in our hearts. A strong heart heals quickly. A healthy friendship makes a heart strong."

Samantha realized that Helly's words were echelons more eloquent than her own. She decided to let her wisdom linger in the moment.

After a while, they each took a deep breath and sat down on the bed. The tension was gone and it felt like clear skies were pushing away storm clouds.

"So, what are you going to do about Hebruce?" Samantha asked.

Helly looked puzzled. "I am not aware of a pending obligation or ritual. Is there something appropriate in American culture for such an occurrence?"

Samantha rolled her eyes and placed her hand on Helly's forearm.

"Oh, Helly. First of all, the guy risked his life to save us. Second of all, he really kicked butt from what I can remember. Lastly, he really cares about you. How you handle this will affect him for the rest of his life."

Helly's eyes widened at the news that she was now liable for the permanent good or harm that could be done to her friend. "I was not aware that this situation possessed such gravity. Are you able to instruct me in the proper manner for such a protocol?"

Samantha smiled, realizing that much was lost in translation. Helly still had not learned that all things teenager contained a high level of drama. She smiled as she put her arm around her friend. "Yes I am."

Maple Ridge Greenway, Richfield

"So, what exactly are we doing here?" Hebruce asked. Samantha had stopped by his house again and asked him to go with her. Technically, this violated the stipulations of her parents' grounding, but after she explained, they once again granted an exception. She was being extremely vague about the details, which was both frustrating and intriguing. Somewhat begrudgingly, he grabbed his mirrored sunglasses and his fur lined coat as they headed toward the park.

As they began to walk toward the fountain, Samantha was tugging at his sleeve to guide him to a particular spot while her eyes excitedly examined her surroundings.

"Alright. Stand right here." Her voice acquired a very serious tone. "Don't move."

He felt a little silly, but hardly anyone was here at this hour of the morning. A few moms were watching their children at the nearby playground. An older lady adorned in a pink jumpsuit and headphones quickly walked by with her arms pumping like a locomotive.

Hebruce stood at the designated spot on the concrete near the fountain. His mind contemplated the possibilities of whatever Samantha had concocted. He wanted to expect something good, but the greater part of him still questioned her decision-making abilities. She had quickly scampered off, leaving him alone. When you're just standing in public, you're never really sure what to do with your hands. He could have shoved them in his pockets or whipped out his phone for some quick scrolling but, instead, he just let them hang as he turned a slow circle to see if anything out of the ordinary caught his eye. Halfway around, something did.

A girl was walking toward him from the rose garden pavilion. She was wearing a white dress with a simple but pretty blue print. Her brown hair was pulled back on the sides but hung down to her shoulders in the back. His physiology involuntarily reacted to the sudden presence of a beautiful girl that he didn't recognize. He straightened his posture, smiled just a little and felt his pulse go up a notch. It didn't immediately process, but something about her was familiar. As she passed under the vine-covered arbor, he suddenly knew who she was.

"Helly?"

She was the same girl he'd ridden bikes and practiced martial arts with, but something was different. He'd never seen her dressed up or her feminine features so accentuated. And she was...smiling. Gone was the blank mask of statuesque emotion. Her expression was warm and her gaze was directed squarely at him. His heartbeat sped up again, so much so that he could feel it thumping in his chest.

She walked straight up to him, placed her hands on each side of his face before leaning in and kissing him on the lips. The times he'd kissed other girls was more like what you'd expect from Hollywood. They had been sloppy and synthetically passionate. This one was simple but had a strange conductivity. A tingle began in his lips and spread throughout his body like electricity. In the moment, he could have committed his life to her.

She gave space but locked eyes with him before she

spoke. "You came to my rescue when I needed you most. That makes you my hero."

His heart was literally pounding as a huge smile spread across his face. This was one of those rare too-good-to-be-true moments that would shape his future. It established an edict in his mind that he would always adhere to, no matter what. You protect what you love. It was this newly engrained truth that would cause fear and even pain to become secondary if the focus of his heart was ever in danger. He was speechless but allowed himself just to relish the experience.

Samantha could keep from spoiling the moment for only so long. A very girlish squeal emanated from her hiding spot near the park map. She was clasping her hands near her mouth and almost dancing with giddiness.

"Oh, you guys!!!" She ran over and pulled her two friends into a huge bear hug. Her coolness still needed some development, but it didn't matter. They wrapped their arms around each other's shoulders, smiles on each face, as they enjoyed another day of youth and life.

When it felt right, they separated and checked on each other. They talked about their parents and also Tom and Mandy. They talked about Matthew and Harmon, including rumors about what was going to happen to them. They swore to never be part of certain activities and pledged their allegiance to one another. In their innocence, none of them realized that even the strongest adolescent bonds can be severed by time and circumstance.

Suddenly, Hebruce's face took on a grave look as if he'd just remembered something important.

"Helly, I almost forgot."

She looked at him, trying to discern what had caused the

sudden change in mood.
    "I received a message."

Hebruce Lee's Home,
520 Pinheel Drive, Richfield

The three of them huddled around Hebruce's laptop. His email account page was open on the screen and he clicked on a message with a subject line of "Who is Helly." The message read:

Hello. I almost didn't send this but the coincidence of it all is just too strange. My son and his wife and little girl disappeared in China fourteen years ago. They were working there as missionaries. In his last letter, he told us that they were relocating to a different part of the country because of political instability. He was concerned about the safety of his family. That was the last time we ever heard from him. The government showed no desire to help us and we could not be transparent about their work there. I'm not sure how to proceed from here but I feel like it's worth it for all of us to investigate this further. I've come to peace with the probability that they are dead, but filling in the blanks would provide a lot of closure. I pray that this is not a cruel hoax. If you have any more information, we would be profoundly grateful. Thank you.

The three of them looked at each other in silence. No one could speak. The magnitude of this possibility could shake the world that they had created over the last three months. Trepidation intermingled with hope and anticipation crept over them all. Wasn't this the whole point of the exposé? Wasn't this what they wanted?

Helly blinked as her mind processed the email. Her words accidentally and inadvertently stung her friends.

"I may not be alone."

John Cleveland

AFTERWORD

Steeped in Shaolin contains some situations that are uncomfortable to say the least. The reason that plane crashes, muggers, would-be rapists, and druggings are included is because these things exist in the real world. The story also contains elements of faith, including Buddhism and Christianity. These were included for the same reasons. Although I strive not to include any profanity or lude content in my writing, I never want my stories to be sanitized to the point of incredulity (where they no longer reflect reality).

Accompanying this malevolence and faith are the worst and best of human attributes. Humans can be short-sighted, selfish, cowardly and even depraved. We can also be sacrificial, honest, courageous and kind. Helly and her circle of friends find themselves teetering between these options on a daily basis. They don't have to go looking for the ultimatums as life tends to drop them directly in their laps. As the story illustrates, even good intentions can result in some horribly messy, complicated and dangerous situations. However, just as it is with life, there is always the opportunity for redemption. Sometimes, it involves internal resolution to protect us from ourselves. At other times, it requires us to lay down our sword and allow ourselves to be carried by another.

My preferred takeaway is that you will be more accepting of your humanity. Show yourself grace and realize that everyone else is probably sorting through the daily barrage of crazy thoughts and emotions just like you are. Use this not as an excuse for complacency but as a motivator to aim higher. Our lives are a process that takes place at what feels like a glacial pace. Most of the time, our progression is seemingly invisible. Then, in an instant, a huge piece of our security falls away into the ocean without warning. If you believe that all of this is happening without any heavenly guidance, I beg you to reconsider.

Please accept my reminder that you matter. The mysterious spark of life that animates you even at this moment is a priceless and temporary gift. Cultivate it, use it, share it, test its limits. Thank you for reading and keep your nunchucks close by for the sequel.

ACKNOWLEDGMENTS

First, giving thanks to God for all things.

Also, I would like to thank my team for reading through previous iterations and giving invaluable insight and feedback.

Lastly, to my sweet wife Shanna for encouraging me and trusting that this exercise in faith will yield fruit for His kingdom.

John Cleveland

ABOUT THE AUTHOR

John Cleveland is an award-winning author known for his first book 40: A Collection of Modern-Day Parables. After serving in the Army Reserves and retiring from the Highway Patrol, he and his wife moved just west of the Rocky Mountains where they enjoy serving their community and exploring God's creation.

For more information about John Cleveland's work, please visit: www.jcwriting.com

John Cleveland

ALSO BY JOHN CLEVELAND

40: A Collection of Modern-Day Parables

Forty short stories about faith, God and human nature. From cruise ships, to electric cars, and even pet dogs, these tales will connect with your heart and soul. Winner of a Christianity Today award.

7: A Sampler from the Larger Collection, "40"

The first seven stories from 40: A Collection of Modern-Day Parables. A small, pocket-sized book that is great to give away as gifts and for events.

The Worst Job Ever (And Why You Should Do It)

A transparent guide for anyone considering a career in law enforcement. It not only covers the basics but gives you an idea of what to expect on patrol and beyond.